HEARTBROKEN

A TALE OF THE ANGRY QUEEN

HEARTBROKEN

A TALE OF THE ANGRY QUEEN

By Serena Valentino

Disney • Hyperion
LOS ANGELES • NEW YORK

Copyright © 2025 by Disney Enterprises, Inc.
All rights reserved. Published by Disney • Hyperion, an
imprint of Buena Vista Books, Inc. No part of this book may
be reproduced or transmitted in any form or by any means,
electronic or mechanical, including photocopying, recording,
or by any information storage and retrieval system, without
written permission from the publisher. For information address
Disney • Hyperion, 7 Hudson Square, New York, New York 10013.

First Edition, July 2025
1st Printing
FAC-004510-25135
Printed in the United States of America

This book is set in 13-point Garamond 3 LT Pro.
Designed by Phil T. Buchanan
Library of Congress Control Number: 2025930342
ISBN 978-1-368-07674-6

Reinforced binding

Visit www.DisneyBooks.com

Logo Applies to Text Stock Only

This book is for my mama. Like the White Rabbit, I have learned time means nothing, and it means everything. And it's impossible to push someone toward joy. All we can do is try to live in joy, and hope those we love will meet us there.

PROLOGUE

From the Book of Fairy Tales

Through the Looking Glass

There are many sorts of looking glasses. Some simply to gaze upon our own faces, while others show us the faces of those we love even when they are in faraway lands. There are mirrors haunted by trapped souls, mirrors that tell us the truth, and mirrors that lie. There are mirrors that allow us to see into other worlds. And if the stars are right, we may even venture into those worlds.

Now that we reside in the Underworld with our beloved Hades, more than ever we rely upon magic mirrors, to speak with our daughter, Circe. Who are we? We are the Odd Sisters, my dears, Lucinda, Ruby, and Martha, the greatest witches of our time, but alas, our time in the realm of the living is now past.

One would think, with her mothers tucked safely away in the Underworld, Circe's reign in the Dead Woods as queen, along with Primrose and Hazel, would be peaceful. However, the Ladies of Light (so named by Hades) have been feeling the vibrations of an ever-more chaotic and increasing magical shift, reverberating not only throughout the Many Kingdoms, but in other lands as well.

If you have been reading the Book of Fairy Tales in the order we've intended, then you too may have noticed these shifts. Unless, of course, you've stumbled upon this volume without reading the stories before it, in which case you will find yourself lost.

Whether you choose to first edify yourself before reading further or stagger down a dangerous and confusing path, what you need to understand is that time means nothing, *and* it means everything. Just ask the White Rabbit. Like us, he knows now all time is happening at once—past, present, and future.

From the Book of Fairy Tales

As you know, the worlds broke when Hades ripped Circe from the place between the living and the dead. And he caused them to shatter even further when he brought us to the Underworld. But it also had an unintended effect, one we were about to discover. Those broken shards of the worlds came together to create a new reality, a terrifyingly beautiful place called Wonderland.

As we would soon learn, Wonderland is a maddening world comprised of fractured shards of other worlds pieced together, as if it were fashioned by a child's wild imaginings. A place where nothing makes sense. A place where time means nothing, yet it means everything. A queendom where a White Rabbit is always late because time is concurrent. And a land where a once serene and happy queen went mad because her existence was literally turned upside down.

There was a time when we thought fate was unavoidable, but now that we see things from a new perspective from the Underworld, we know both time and fate are fluid, because there is no past or future. Just look at the work Circe, Hazel, and Primrose are doing, how they intend to change the fates of those in the Book of Fairy Tales who have been wronged by our meddling. However, we have come to the sobering conclusion that this is our responsibility, and not our daughter's. It became clear to us the moment we walked into the hall of mirrors and saw the ramifications caused by Hades changing our fates by bringing us to the Underworld.

In Hades's hall of mirrors, there are looking glasses that see into every world, and when we say every world, we mean even yours. When Hades broke the worlds with his magic, some of these mirrors shattered as well. The shards broke away, fusing together to create a new world. This is one of the many ways worlds are made. Something from nothing, and sometimes something from everything. It's happened before and will happen again.

When we walk through the hall of mirrors, we see the missing pieces. We see the parts that have broken away to create new worlds, and pieces that have simply disappeared. We see the shard that contains what looks like a whimsical forest but hosts a dark and dangerous creature. A tiny sliver that is from a land in perpetual unbirthday celebrations. We see the jagged pieces of other kingdoms ruled by White and Red Queens (perhaps, then, they are queendoms), and pieces from lands where it is not unusual for mice, caterpillars, rabbits, and cats to speak. And a land where a little girl falls asleep under the trees in the park when she should be at her studies.

There are only two mirrors in Hades's hall of mirrors that do not have missing or misplaced pieces: the Many Kingdoms, and the Underworld.

But we fear that might not always be so, especially with what's to come. If the realms within the Many Kingdoms go to war, we fear another breaking of the worlds, and this time we are not sure if the Many Kingdoms will be spared. And what land will be lost if shards of the Many Kingdoms break away? Will it be Queen Snow White's realm, Queen Belle's? Or will it be the Dead Woods? We cannot fathom. What is certain is that more fractures will break away

Heartbroken

if Circe is unable to stop Tulip and her army of Tree Lords and Cyclopean Giants from attacking the Beast King's castle.

As it stands, Circe and the other ladies of the Dead Woods are bound in blood to help their allies when they call for aid. And Tulip knew that when she called upon the Queens of the Dead. The Dead Woods has a long history, steeped in blood, magic, and violence. However, when Circe, Primrose, and Hazel took their thrones as queens of the once bleak and loathsome place, they decided to make it their own, to fill it with life and light. They knew they could never erase the dreadful and unspeakable acts of the past, but they were determined to undo the harm caused by the queens, witches, and fairies who came before them. And most especially the harm caused by us.

Circe never dreamed Queen Tulip would declare war on the Beast King, even if he caused Tulip unspeakable heartbreak before he redeemed himself through his love for Belle. But before Belle, he was not the man or king he is today. He broke many hearts, including the heart of Tulip, who was so heartbroken by his cruelty to her and her kingdom of Morningstar, she threw herself on the cliffs of her father's shores into the water below. There, she found herself making a deal with the sea witch Ursula, who gave Tulip her life back in exchange for her beauty and her voice. Since those dark days Tulip has remade herself, and has become a strong woman with a purpose.

Yet Circe never fathomed what Tulip's true purpose was while spending her time with the Tree Lords, the giant trees of the ancient forests, and Cyclopean rock giants; she never imagined Tulip was readying for war, and revenge on the Beast King. She never fathomed she would find herself obliged to raise her own undead army to do battle for any reason other than self-defense. But the new Queens of the Dead, renamed the Ladies of Light, had pledged their allegiance to Queen Tulip years before, an oath made in blood, which is unbreakable and magically binding. It was an easy promise for the Ladies of Light to make at the time. They trusted Tulip; she was, after all, their family and friend. It never occurred to Circe that Tulip had been plotting against the Beast King over these many years that had passed since his grievous transgressions against her, which are chronicled in their shared stories *The Beast Within* and *Kill the Beast* within this Book of Fairy Tales.

But it did occur to us. We saw it coming. We knew Queen Tulip would expect the ladies of the Dead Woods to join their army with hers and march on the Beast King's castle. To destroy him, if need be, and anyone who stood in her path.

Anyone who wasn't expecting this hasn't been paying attention. Anyone who wonders why now, after all this time, still doesn't understand that time means nothing, *and* it means everything.

Tulip knows this well. She knew it all along. She spent years with the great Tree Lord Oberon and his ilk, exploring the dark and light forests, learning ancient magic known only to the entities of the woods. She took the time she knew she had, amassing an unfathomably large legion of Tree Lords and Cyclopeans in secret, and without the notice of the Ladies of Light. Tulip crept into the oldest forests and woke the trees that had been slumbering for more years than anyone could recollect using ancient magic even we did not know existed, and she rallied them all to her cause.

But this was not the only trouble brewing in the Many Kingdoms. Not long before Tulip's declaration of war, the Ladies of Light received a letter from Snow White asking for their help. All she would say was there was something wrong with her stepmother's old enchanted mirror and to please come to her as soon as they were able, but Circe and the other queens of the Dead Woods were distracted by what would seem to be an endless siege of unfortunate events that may prove to be too much for the young queens to deal with on their own.

What has this to do with the Queen of Hearts? Everything, and nothing.

If you've read the previous stories in this Book of

Fairy Tales, then you know everything is connected, and Tulip's war was not the only event that threatened to put those in the Many Kingdoms in peril. But something even more disturbing than war and the haunting of Snow White's mirror was brewing in a distant land of our own creation, and it was putting everything, and everyone, at risk. And this is that story.

Her story. The story of the angry queen.

CHAPTER I

THE QUEEN OF HEARTS

The Queen of Hearts often mused it might have been better if it hadn't happened all at once. Perhaps then it wouldn't be so maddening. But it did happen all at once, or at least it seemed so to the Queen, finding herself in such an unfamiliar, bewildering, and overwhelming land.

In Wonderland she was surrounded by noise, chaos, riddles, and strangers, yet somehow these strangers called her their Queen, a notion that initially gave her more than a little pause. But surely she had always been queen, had she not? And if not of this place, surely somewhere else. However, the more she thought of it, the more convinced she became she hadn't always been the Queen of Wonderland. Not this maddening, bewildering, and confounding kingdom that was so puzzling, and yet so oddly familiar, surrounded by bothersome inhabitants who seemed to go out of their way to vex and befuddle her. Somehow she was expected to be their Queen, and to hold her temper. Which seemed impossible, being surrounded by so much madness.

She could hardly recall what her life was before she found herself in Wonderland. Only a sense that there had once been happiness and everything made sense. She was sure her life once had rules, and order. And now there was nothing but chaos. Nothing made sense, and she was angry all the time.

Even though it had been many years since she woke up to this new life of hers, it still felt like it had all been some horrible mistake, like she didn't belong. And the fact was, she had no desire to fit in, or belong in such a maddening land. She just wanted to escape.

At first she struggled against it; she tried to quell the thunderous anger that lived inside her, but

The Queen of Hearts

nothing she did helped, not for long, anyway, and now it seemed it was too late. The noise around her, and in her head, was cacophonous. The anger was too enormous, and there was only one thing left to do. She had to kill everyone in Wonderland. Maybe then she would have peace.

This perfect and sublime conclusion had come to the Queen one morning as she sat drinking her tea and mindlessly picking at a plate of her favorite cookies, and it made her giddy. She laughed like a woman possessed as she rushed to her desk, where she took out her stationery and quill to write out the invitations. She would have a party! A party in which everyone would die.

She was giddy at the thought of lopping off everyone's heads. It was what kings and queens did, was it not? At least, that was what the White Rabbit had told her on one of his many dissertations about the habits of monarchs. It would seem if they were displeased with someone's behavior, they simply chopped off their heads. And to the Queen, some of their reasons were rather frivolous, but she knew *she* was justified. She couldn't wait to see their stupid heads lying on the floor with vapid, lifeless expressions. Then and only then would there be no more riddles or insipid stories tripping off their lips; no more unbirthday songs, or tall tales, or petty squabbling. The only thing that would be pouring from their mouths would be blood. She was surprised by the pure bliss these images sent through her body, imagining their crimson blood streaked across the floors. As she sealed the last envelope, she sighed with relief, experiencing the first glimmer of peace she had felt since she first found herself in Wonderland. Soon they would all have their invitations. Soon they would all die.

Fueled by inspiration, she seized the large brass bell that was sitting on her writing desk and rang it furiously until one of her maids came shuffling into the room. She was a slight, timid young woman, with big eyes, dark hair tucked into her maid's cap, and a black uniform with red heart embellishments. She was trembling when she entered the room. The Queen could see her hands shake and her lips

The Queen of Hearts

quivering, and she wondered if the maid would give her an excuse to behead her. Only time would tell.

"Take these invitations to the White Rabbit immediately! Tell him he is to deliver every single one of them before he attends upon me at our usual time today. And inform the staff we will be hosting a lavish party for all of my subjects, and tell them to make haste! I want everything done without delay! Cakes, cookies, refreshments, decorations, games, no excuses!" she said, throwing the bell at the poor maid, who scrambled out of the room. The Queen didn't care if this was an impossible task for her already harried servants. Really, what did it matter? Soon they would all be dead.

As it was, the Queen already had her cooks and bakers working around the clock, making every delight imaginable just in case she or the King should fancy it. Everyone in her court knew the penalty if the Queen didn't get what she wanted, exactly when she demanded it. And it wasn't as if she had a small household; counting herself and the King, there were fifty-two of them—well, fifty-three, actually, if you counted the White Rabbit, give or take a few beheadings. So there were no excuses.

But when she thought about it, that number, fifty-two, was curious. Something felt familiar, yet so distant in her memories that were now somehow shrouded in darkness. When she first found herself in Wonderland, she tried to reach into that darkness, to grab on to something of her time before, but she would find herself feeling even more confused and bewildered than before. So eventually she gave up. She stopped trying to remember. Still, everything about her life, then and now, remained a conundrum.

You would think the talking cats, caterpillars, and rabbits of Wonderland, or the number fifty-two, would be the pressing mystery. But that wasn't the case. It was her overwhelming anger. From the moment she woke up in Wonderland, she was teetering between confusion and anger. And the more confused she became, the more intense the anger. As time went on, it was as if the rage of not just one but *three* women resided within her. She was in constant misery and on the verge of collapse. It was exhausting

The Queen of Hearts

to be so angry all the time, to have so much hate bubbling inside her, like a pot of jam boiling over on the stove. Leaving a mess for others to clean up so she didn't have to face her own misery.

As she looked around the morning room, the room in which she spent most mornings and afternoons, she wished she could be happy. She felt selfish, and broken, as if she didn't know how to be happy even surrounded by such lovely things and a staff that was always there to give her whatever she wished. But she wasn't happy. It didn't matter how beautiful or comfortable her castle was, or if her gardens were filled with her favorite flowers, or if she had a doting husband. She hated her life, because she hated being in Wonderland.

As she looked down at the plate of her favorite cookies, round and white with a red heart jam center, she became aggrieved they weren't cake. She looked around for her bell, then remembered she had thrown it at the maid and decided she had no other choice but to bellow as loudly as she could.

"Bring me some cake! And not one of those

infernal unbirthday cakes!" she yelled, making a note to herself that she needed more than one bell.

Her voice boomed through the cavernous room, making her servants scatter wildly, knocking into each other and bouncing off of walls before scurrying off to the kitchen for her cake. She would have laughed, but she couldn't. Nothing but anger lived within her these days, and sometimes she would marvel at herself, surprised at how much she had changed since she'd first arrived. She missed the days of laughing, and inquisitiveness. She missed the days of wonder, when she wandered this strange land searching for answers and friends, when it was easier to keep her worst impulses in check. She missed trying to figure out the mysteries of her kingdom, and how excited she was to meet her subjects and learn their stories. But those days were long past.

All that remained was the anger.

As she sat there munching the last of her cookies, anxiously awaiting the cake, she tried to remember the exact moment when the anger became her world, and when this insatiable need for cake overtook her.

The Queen of Hearts

It was odd how frequently she craved it now, how eating it seemed to make the anger subside, if only momentarily, and she wondered why she hadn't asked for it first thing that morning. Just then a servant appeared in the room with a fresh plate of her favorite cookies, and not the cake she desperately needed. She felt herself growing more infuriated, the heat rising in her cheeks, her knuckles turning white as her nails dug into her palms. It took everything within her not to kill the servant right there on the spot. Though she hardly knew why she hadn't done so.

"I said cake! I want cake! Bring me cake or I will have your head!" The servant placed the cookies on the Queen's side table with shaking hands, and her eyes filled with a mixture of fear and confusion. But the servant's confusion was nothing compared to the Queen's.

Even she did not understand it, this desire, this need for cake. Sometimes when no one was looking she would shove fistfuls of cake into her mouth, stuffing herself until she felt sick. But it was the only thing that made her feel better. The only thing

Heartbroken

that dampened her rage. She knew something was desperately wrong. It was more than maddening, it was terrifying. The flashing images of her previous life seemed to fade by the day. Now when she tried to recall, she saw only darkness, and she didn't dare reach into that darkness because she was too afraid of what might be lingering there.

But even more unnerving were the voices in her head. Not just her own, but other women, too. Three other women, to be precise. But the worst thing of all was that she was sure the anger belonged to them, and it was they who demanded the cake.

The thought of it made her feel as if she were losing her senses. To even think such a thing made her feel foolish. She daren't tell anyone about these women, not even her closest confidant, the White Rabbit. Everyone would think she was mad from her long years of confinement. But then, wasn't everyone in Wonderland mad? Perhaps they, too, heard these woman's voices, the screeching laughter echoing in their minds, making them all mad.

She had spent too long wondering about these

The Queen of Hearts

mysterious women. Wondering how to escape their madness. But there was no escape. Not from them, and not from Wonderland. And there was only one thing left for the Queen to do. Perhaps then she would have peace.

She was so long in her thoughts that she hardly noticed her husband, the King, when he came into the room. Then again, she hardly noticed him most of the time as it was. How small and strange he looked to her, how odd, and jolly. There was something comical about him in his oversize kingly outfit, almost like a child dressing up in his father's clothing. His robe dragged on the floor, collecting cookie crumbs as he crossed the room, and the Queen wondered if the maids knew how much easier their jobs were due to their diminutive king sweeping his way through the castle. He noticed the bell lying on the floor, casually picked it up, and placed it on the Queen's desk, as if it was the most normal thing in the world.

"I see the maid was annoying you again," he said, sitting down on the red loveseat. The Queen could tell he wanted her to sit beside him, but she was happy at her desk. Even if it didn't show on his face, she knew it hurt him when she didn't move to join him. He always had the same smile plastered across his face no matter what was going on. The more disgusted she was with him, the wider he smiled. Nothing ever seemed to bother him. He was immune to the madness of Wonderland, to the Queen's anger, to the voices. The castle could fall down around them and he'd still be smiling.

The fact was, she couldn't stand the sight of the King, or the sound of his voice chattering away at her about the absurd goings-on in their queendom. It mattered not to her that the Mock Turtle told his story again, or that those fatuous Tweedle brothers were waylaying travelers on the road with their impossible riddles and platitudes. What did she care if the Caterpillar had once again been rude, or the Mad Hatter perpetually thought it was teatime, or some oysters were tricked into being eaten, again and again, never learning from their mistakes? During all her years of imprisonment, nothing had changed. Everything had remained the same, and somehow it

The Queen of Hearts

was more intolerable than ever. The only thing that brought her peace was knowing she would have all of their heads. All of them. Every single one of them. Perhaps even the King's.

"My love, are you listening?" the King asked, taking a cookie from the plate and eating it. She was disgusted by the crumbs falling onto his robes and the jam that stuck to his teeth as he smacked his lips. How did she find herself married to such a simpering fool of a man? In what world, under what circumstances, could she have ever agreed to marry him? She certainly had no memory of choosing to do so. As she sat there looking at him, she couldn't fathom it, and when she searched her mind for possible reasons, it only drove her to distraction. So instead she imagined his head lying lifeless on the floor, his blood pooling around him and his face stuck in a perpetual smile.

"Of course I'm not listening to you, my dear. What is it now? Let me guess, a walrus doing a dance? Or perhaps the Mad Hatter thought he lost his Dormouse again, only to find it sleeping in a teapot? Or the Duchess's cat is up to its tricks again?"

She was still imagining his severed head, and it almost made her laugh.

"No, no, no! It's the little girl! Everyone in Wonderland is talking about her." This was new. The first new thing in Wonderland that she could recall. The Queen sat up straighter. She might even have been interested.

"What little girl? We don't have a little girl! I have not seen, nor heard of a single little girl in all of Wonderland!"

"We have one now. She's been running all over the queendom, introducing herself to everyone she encounters. Her name is Alice."

"Alice? What a grotesque name. What insolence! Introducing herself to everyone in the queendom before she comes to greet the Queen? How dare she?"

"Well, to be fair, I did hear she didn't immediately introduce herself to the Tweedles . . ." the King began, but the Queen was not listening. Instead she looked at the clock, ticking closer to the hour at hand. The hour in which the White Rabbit was expected to return. The Queen smiled as she watched

The Queen of Hearts

the second hand moving along, savoring the image of the rabbit panicking, racing through the castle out of breath, muttering "I am late" as he passed scrambling servants. And right on time, at the precise moment he was expected, the White Rabbit appeared, out of breath and quivering with nerves. She almost took delight in seeing him in such a state, all for the sake of pleasing her with his punctuality. Of all her subjects, the White Rabbit was the only one in the queendom who did, occasionally, manage to please her. She didn't imagine him headless. She wondered if she should spare him. Someone, after all, would have to clean up the blood.

"Have you delivered all the invitations, Rabbit? Every last one?" She didn't look at the rabbit, she kept her eyes fixed on the door, eagerly awaiting the servants with her cake. Had she been looking at the White Rabbit, she would have seen he was more anxious than ever. But she needn't look, she could hear his heavy breathing and the nervousness in his voice. She almost felt sorry for him.

"Yes, my Queen, I delivered all of the invitations.

Heartbroken

All but one," said the trembling rabbit. The Queen whipped her head in his direction in anger.

"Which one? Who didn't receive their invitation? How dare you not deliver all of the invitations? Every single person, animal, pig baby, walking chess piece, as well as any other puerile being in this infernal kingdom must attend! Every single one! Do you understand?" The Queen was enraged, and she wouldn't be able to rest until all of them were dead. The thought of just one of those insane creatures running around Wonderland made her skin crawl. No, they must all die. All of them. Perhaps even the White Rabbit.

"The one for the little girl. I've come to understand her name is Alice, Your Majesty. She followed me all over. At first I thought she was my maid, Mary-Ann. But Mary-Ann would never grow to impossible heights and destroy my house, or scare the Dormouse, or confound the hatter and March Hare with riddles about a raven."

"Stop this senseless chatter immediately, Rabbit!

The Queen of Hearts

I refuse to listen to Wonderland nonsense!" said the Queen.

"Of course, Your Majesty. The point is, I didn't see an invitation for Alice with the others."

"Well, of course you didn't—she doesn't live here, you fool of a rabbit! Where in Wonderland would you deliver it? No matter, you make sure she finds her way here today. MAKE SURE THEY ALL DO." She despised her own booming voice, resentful that she couldn't control the anger.

"I daresay it might be a challenge to get everyone here with so little notice. Your subjects can be rather eccentric, and high-spirited—"

"And dead." The rabbit jumped, startled at the Queen's words. "That is, they *will be dead* if they don't attend," she continued before he could reply. "Tell them without their heads there will be no more tomfoolery, leapfrogging, silly dances, or absurd riddles. Tell them without their heads they will no longer be able to drink tea, or eat cake, or ask rude questions. Because, dear Rabbit, that will be the penalty for anyone who doesn't attend my party today. Make sure they know."

"I believe it said so on the invitation, Your Majesty," said the White Rabbit. "Everyone in the kingdom is aware."

"Very well, very well, but will it make my nonsensical subjects attend? They must all come!" She was digging her nails into the palms of her hands again, this time so hard she drew blood. A droplet of scarlet fell to the floor, and a lovely feeling washed over her as she imagined the White Queen's head lying in a pool of the same color. She laughed aloud, and the White Rabbit jumped. He was especially twitchy this day. More like a rabbit.

"They, are, as you say, *eccentric*, Your Majesty," he said, giving her the side-eye.

Eccentric was an understatement. Everyone in Wonderland was insane. And it made the Queen wonder if this was all her fault. She couldn't remember what came first: all these maddening distractions, or her temper? Surely her temper was a result of this increasing mania that seemed to seize their queendom.

But was her temper making it worse, was it causing her subjects to act more erratically, and even more annoyingly? It was a cycle she felt she couldn't break, and she was left with only one solution.

Off with their heads!

"She is almost here, my Queen." The White Rabbit interrupted her thoughts so suddenly that she couldn't remember what they had been talking about.

"Who? Who is almost here? What are you going on about now?" She shook her head, trying to clear her mind of the maniacal laughter. It was so loud, and so overwhelming, she was convinced everyone must also hear it. For all she knew, everyone else was sane and she was the one who was mad. They all had similar dispositions, even if their particular brands of peculiarities were rather distinct. The one thing they did share was their penchant for nonsense.

"The little girl, my Queen. *Alice.* She is almost here."

"Of course! Yes! The little girl! Right. Well then, Rabbit, see to it the servants ready the croquet pitch, and sharpen the royal ax!" She pushed past her tiny husband, almost knocking him over. The White Rabbit's whiskers twitched in amusement. He disliked the King almost as much as she did. He was after all rather useless, just standing there in silence munching away at an entire plate of cookies.

"And ready the flamingos! And round up the hedgehogs, and all the other nonsense one needs in this damnable place to play croquet. We will have our party in the garden, and little Alice will join us!" She threw up her hands dramatically, emboldened that her plans were being set in motion.

"Yes! A garden party! That's the perfect place." Once everyone was beheaded, she and the White Rabbit could use their heads as croquet balls. Oh, how wonderful that would be, to knock their heads around the garden. The thought of it made her laugh, and for a moment she felt happy, to laugh with the strange women in her head, to join them rather than being tormented by them.

"Oh yes, Your Majesty! The garden is the perfect place!" The White Rabbit met her eye, as if he had

The Queen of Hearts

some notion of her bloody daydreams. As if he knew what she was planning.

"What do you know of perfect places for a garden party? *What do you know*, Little Rabbit?" she asked, narrowing her eyes at him and wondering if he knew what she had planned. Then she remembered. Of course he knew! Of anyone in the kingdom the White Rabbit knew her best.

"Well, if one is going to have a garden party, the garden *does* seem like the perfect location," said the rabbit, eyeing her.

"Indeed!" she said as two servants came into the room with an enormous cake on a tea cart. It was by far the largest cake they had made her so far, and every layer was frosted in a different color. She smiled as she beheld the two servants standing on either side of the cake, their faces stricken by fear as they waited to see if she would approve of the baker's handiwork. It seemed from the very first day she appeared in Wonderland she was cast in a role she had been destined to play. A part she never wanted, and had only recently decided to embrace. The part of the angry Queen.

"Too late! Too late! The cake has come too late! Off with their heads!" she said as she took a handful, shoved it in her mouth, and flung the frosting from her fingers at the poor servants who were frozen in horror. *Oh yes, this is satisfying. Cake and death,* she thought as she looked down at the servants, who were on their knees begging her for mercy.

"Oh don't look at me like that. You know the penalty! Off with your heads!" The guards came into the room to drag the servants off to the courtyard for their beheadings. She smiled and took another bite of cake as the servants' screams filled the halls. She delighted in the fear she could hear in their voices, calling to her over and over, pleading with her to change her mind. But even more blissful was the silence that came afterward.

Yes, cake and death, they make this dreadful place almost tolerable, she thought, before remembering the rabbit was standing there waiting for her to dismiss him.

The Queen of Hearts

"Oh, and White Rabbit. I hope you don't think I forgot to invite *you* to my garden party. Though I daresay it hardly makes sense to have you deliver the invitation to yourself. So here." She took a white envelope from her pocket and handed it to him.

"It will be my—my . . . honor to attend, my Queen," said the rabbit.

Oh yes, of course the White Rabbit remembers. He knows my plan.

Chapter II

The White Gentlerabbit

On the day the White Rabbit first met the Queen of Hearts, she was within the castle grounds climbing over a tall hedge in her elaborate garden labyrinth. This was a great many years before she decided to behead everyone in her kingdom. A great many years before she was overcome with bloodlust and rage.

On that day in the hedge maze the White Rabbit must have startled the Queen of Hearts, because when he said hello she squealed and toppled backward over the hedge. He heard a loud thud, followed by a penetrating scream that made his whiskers twitch. The rabbit quickly scampered around the long hedge to find the Queen sprawled upon the labyrinthine path. Her outer skirt had flipped up over her face, exposing the black-and-yellow underskirt, numerous petticoats, white stockings, and silk shoes beneath. It was a curious sight: this woman he had never seen before covered in bits of leaves from the shrubbery, uttering muffled curses from under the thick red-and-black velvet dress that was covering her face.

The last thing the White Rabbit wanted was to embarrass the Queen (for surely that was who she must have been) by staring at her in such a state, so he promptly turned away. Better that he let her smarten herself up before he made his introductions. He had heard rumors throughout the kingdom of a new queen. Or at least, he *thought* he had. Come to think of it, he wasn't sure if he had met anyone in the kingdom aside from the Queen. He wasn't sure if he really had heard such a thing, or, if he had, when or where he had heard it. He didn't even know if there had been a previous queen, and, if there had, where she had gone or how it came to be they had a new one. There was a lot he didn't know. When a brief moment passed in which he thought he did know something, then he would wonder how he knew it. Just like how he thought he had heard they had a new queen.

He found it all rather strange, the not remembering. It was as if he had woken up and this was his first day here—wherever *here* was. But how could it be? He supposed it didn't matter if he had always been in this strange land or just happened to appear there that day, or if he would eventually find himself somewhere else. What mattered was this very moment. Yes, this was the only moment that mattered; to think too much about the hows and whys would only make him go mad.

And so it was in this particular moment he was almost sure he had heard a rumor about a new queen. Even if he didn't know who had told him this rumor. What mattered now was that the Queen was lying on the path before him covered in dirt, twigs, and bits of leaves. He was too small to help her to her feet—he was, after all, rabbit size, at least he thought so—and the best course of action was to find someone who was bigger than he. Yes, that was the best plan. But

The White Gentlerabbit

then it occurred to him it might be rude just to walk away, leaving her sprawled in the dirt, and decided it was probably best to say *something*.

Still with his back to the Queen, making sure to give her the dignity he was sure she probably deserved, he said, "Are you quite all right, my Queen? Shall I get someone to help?" The truth was he wasn't sure what she deserved, as he had only just laid eyes on her, and she was upside down with her dress over her head, but he was a gentlerabbit, after all—at least, he thought he was. And gentlerabbits always did the right thing if it was in their power to do so.

"Since I see no one else in this maze but you, Little White Rabbit, I assume it is you who is speaking to me now?" said the Queen. Her voice sounded less muffled, which made the rabbit think she was now at least sitting up, but of course he couldn't be sure without turning around.

"Indeed. Would you prefer that I not speak?" he asked.

"You may speak. And explain why you are calling me your Queen," said the Queen, which seemed like a very odd question to the rabbit. It was plain to see she was the Queen, and not just because of the rumors he may or may not have heard. She was, in fact, on the castle grounds, and she was dressed in a queenly manner, and she did seem to have a queenly air about her. Surely she was the Queen. It had never occurred to him she wasn't the Queen. Though he did wonder why a queen would climb a hedge, but that seemed like an impertinent question, and gentlerabbits didn't ask impertinent questions, unless they had to.

"Because you are the Queen," he said simply and with confidence.

"Am I? Oh! Well then, you may turn around." He did so, to see her standing there, all evidence of her misadventure now gone. As the rabbit looked at her more closely, he decided she couldn't have been anyone else but the Queen, especially now that she was upright, and her dress was, by anyone's estimation, a dress that couldn't have been worn by anyone other than a queen, or a person pretending to be a queen, though he found that highly unlikely.

The White Gentlerabbit

"And how is it that I find myself standing in a hedge maze talking to a White Rabbit wearing a little waistcoat, and holding an ill-proportioned pocket watch, and rabbit-size bumbershoot? It's strange, is it not?"

"I don't know, Your Majesty." The fact was, he wasn't sure what was strange and what wasn't. But if he were forced to decide, he would say nothing about his person or ensemble was strange.

"And I suppose you don't know how you came across a rabbit-size bumbershoot? You'd think if such a thing existed then a proper-size pocket watch wouldn't be too much to ask for. Then again, I have never to my knowledge encountered a talking rabbit, so I suppose nothing here makes sense," she said with a cheeky smile. It never occurred to him to wonder where he had gotten his pocket watch or why it was so large. All he knew was that he needed it to make sure he got to his appointments on time, though what appointments those were, he didn't know. As for the bumbershoot, well that was another story, which made sense to him. Surely he'd gotten it from the same place he procured his suit, even if he couldn't recall where that might have been.

"Considering I have no memory of how I came here, or how I came into the possession of my things, I couldn't say." He surprised himself in saying it aloud. It was true, he didn't remember much of anything, but admitting it, to a queen, no less, seemed to make it all the more real.

"Don't you? How odd, neither do I. Not in any real sense, anyway. Do you suppose there is a reason why, or if someone here would know? Someone who could solve this riddle?" the Queen asked, looking around in sort of a daze as if she had no idea how she found herself in such an enormous hedge maze, or how she found herself in this place at all. But it was easy for him to come to this conclusion, not only by the look on her face but because he was feeling the same way.

"I have no idea, but I wouldn't mind if you wanted to discover the mystery of this place together," said the rabbit.

The White Gentlerabbit

"I wonder . . ." said the Queen, looking around. "I don't even know what to call this land. Perhaps we will find its name on our adventure."

"I'm sure we will," said the White Rabbit. He glanced at his pocket watch nervously.

"Do you have somewhere to be, Little Rabbit? Am I keeping you from an important appointment?"

"I don't think so, Your Majesty. I believe I am exactly where I'm supposed to be."

"I wish I could say the same." The Queen looked sad to the White Rabbit in that moment, so bewildered and confused. So lost. So unlike the Queen she would become.

"May I ask why you were climbing over the hedge?" He was feeling a bit braver now that the Queen seemed like a reasonable person, and in quite the same predicament as he.

"I was afraid," she said. "But never mind all that, Little Rabbit. I have a feeling we are going to be good friends. I like you. And if I have to be trapped in a strange place, it might as well be with you."

"Trapped, Your Majesty?"

Heartbroken

"Haven't you noticed, my dear little friend? There is no way out of this wonderland. No way out at all. That's why I was afraid."

"Are you sure, Your Majesty?" The rabbit wondered how she knew this since neither of them seemed to have explored the land beyond this hedge maze and therefore couldn't possibly know what way was in or out, or if there was a way in or out at all.

"I suppose I'm not sure, Rabbit. I think it's just a feeling. A dreadful, foreboding, dire feeling. And if I were to be entirely honest, it makes me a bit angry as well." In that moment, she looked less like a queen and more like a lost little girl surrounded by tall hedges she couldn't find her way through.

"Then it seems we have two objectives," he said, with a lilt to his voice that he hoped would embolden her. "We will find out the mysteries of this place, and if we don't like them, we will find a way out."

"Indeed! Now, let's get out of here before my husband tracks me down," she said dramatically, moving her eyes to the left as if she were trying to ascertain if he was in pursuit of her, when both of them knew

The White Gentlerabbit

very well he was not since there was no sign of anyone on the grounds, let alone a king. This made the rabbit laugh. He liked this woman, he liked her a lot. She was funny, and playful, and quick-witted. Just the sort of person he'd like to call friend.

"Husband, Your Majesty?" It hadn't occurred to the rabbit the Queen would have a husband. But then again, in most cases when there was a queen there was also a king. The rabbit wondered why that was so, and how it was he knew such a thing. And then he wondered why two kings or two queens couldn't rule the land. Or perhaps just one queen. Surely this wasn't uncommon. And if it was, it shouldn't be.

"Yes, Rabbit, my husband, the King. That is who I was running from when I found myself in the maze."

"Is he a horrible, beastly man, then?"

"No. I just don't remember being married to him. Can you imagine waking up and turning over to find a stranger in your bed? Well, I assume it was my bed. And to me he was a stranger. I have no idea, honestly. Oh, I'm sure you think I'm mad. Well, I'm not, I tell you, I am not mad! I have never laid eyes on this man before, this supposed husband of mine. At least, I don't think I have. And if I have, I don't recall ever being married to him, even though it is customary for kings and queens to be married, I suppose. But I tell you, I've never seen this castle, or these grounds, or the land that lies beyond it." The rabbit was surprised by how quickly her fear turned to anger. But who could blame her, really? So far, her day had been far more frightening than he imagined.

"Today must be your first day," he said, smiling at her, trying to de-escalate her emotions. Something he would come to do more often as time passed.

"What do you mean, *first day?*"

The rabbit could see a spark of curiosity flashing in her eyes, even if she was still a bit panicked.

"Everyone's story has to start somewhere, doesn't it? And it seems our stories start today, right here in this hedge maze. Why not make the most of it?" he asked earnestly, for her sake as well as his own. He meant every word.

He knew in that moment it was up to him to help the Queen, not only to find out everything they could about this place, but to help her stay calm. The fact was, he wasn't sure how he was able to remain so calm himself, why he wasn't panicking. But he was happy he wasn't, and he felt it was his duty to make sure the Queen didn't panic, either, because he caught on very early in their acquaintance, and eventual friendship, that her anger was rooted in fear, panic, and an inability to escape the very environment that caused her to feel those things. He could tell she was a woman who felt deeply. She felt her joy and anger in equal measure, and needed someone to steer her toward joy.

"But what of all the other days that came before today? Where are they?" the Queen asked with a bewildered and frightened look on her face.

"They're behind us. Or maybe in front of us. Who knows? All that matters is today," he said with a confidence he felt suited him well. He couldn't be sure, of course, if this had always been his personality, but he decided it would be from this point forward.

"Are you sure?"

"Quite sure, Your Majesty. So what if we don't

remember who we were yesterday? What matters is who we are today." The moment he said it, he knew it was true. At least, it was true for him. All he needed was to convince the Queen this was the way to look at things.

"But I don't even know who I am today!"

"Think of it this way: by all indications it would seem you *are* the Queen, and therefore we can conclude you rule this land. That's a good start, don't you think?"

"That's a very good start," she said, her smile returning.

"And as your subject, I am at your whim. What shall we make our first order of business?" He was happy his words seemed to be giving her courage, happy her panic and fear were diminishing.

"Perhaps we should bake a bunch of cakes?" she asked with a cheeky smirk.

"Cakes, Your Majesty?"

"Yes, cakes. Something is telling me the best way to introduce ourselves to our neighbors is to bring them a cake."

The White Gentlerabbit

"Your subjects, Your Majesty, not your neighbors. Best to think of them that way."

"Yes, yes! But isn't it the best idea?" she asked, clasping her hands like a little girl pleading for treats with wide eyes and an impish smile. He liked this side of her. There was something sweet and innocent about the Queen in her moments of joy, which instantly endeared her to the White Rabbit.

"It is an interesting notion, Your Majesty, but is it wise or seemly for a queen to go door-to-door, passing out cakes? Shouldn't you send out an invitation for your subjects to come to you?" The rabbit wasn't sure why his plan seemed more sensible. Why shouldn't a queen visit each of her subjects and give them gifts if she liked? But there was something within him that said such things were just not done, and the best course was to have her subjects come to her. But more than this notion of breaking protocol, there was something else within him that urged him against this plan, a fear that it would set them down a dangerous road from which they might not return.

"I suppose there is wisdom in that. You are a good

advisor, Little Rabbit. How do you know so much about how queens should conduct themselves?" She looked as if she were contemplating his advice and deciding what she would like to do. As the rabbit would soon learn, more times than not the Queen would do exactly as she pleased, even though she was almost always willing to listen to his suggestions.

"I don't know," he said, realizing it was true. He wasn't sure how he knew the manner in which queens should conduct themselves, or why he was sure it was better if her subjects came to her. He supposed it was just a matter of common sense, not that he would say so to her. No matter how friendly they had become in such a short period, the last thing he would do is imply the Queen lacked common sense.

"Do you think this is how all queens are made, Little Rabbit? Do they all wake up one day and find that they are a queen? Seems like an odd way to go about things." She spoke as if she thought he had the answer. And he supposed that did seem like something he should know. The fact was, he didn't know how queens were made. It seemed to him it was something queens were born to be, and his Queen, the one standing before him, struck him as a woman who had always been Queen. It hadn't occurred to him she hadn't been a queen before she came to find herself in Wonderland.

"Are you suggesting you don't think you were a queen before?"

"Before what?"

"Before today."

"I suppose I must have been. I have the dress, and I am married to the King." She looked off into the distance as if she were struggling to remember something but it was too far away and no amount of squinting would allow her to see it in her mind's eye. But then, for just a moment, it was as if her eyes sparked, and the rabbit could see that at last the Queen remembered something.

"I do have memories of large parties with other kings, queens, and knaves. I can hear the sound of laughter surrounding us, happy voices, and glasses tinkling. I can picture firelight dancing on the walls around us. Then suddenly, everything ends, and there is nothing, only blackness. And all is quiet and calm until we are brought back into the light again, and then the laughter starts all over. Does that make sense to you, Little Rabbit? It doesn't make sense to me."

"Perhaps the darkness is just the missing parts of your memory," said the White Rabbit.

"Perhaps. And perhaps that is why, as you said, today is the only day that matters. *Our first day.* Oh, I like the sound of that! First day! Should we see if there is anyone in this castle of mine who can bake some cakes? Do you think there is such a person?"

"I'm sure there is, Your Majesty."

"And since I am the Queen, and I make the rules, I say we deliver the cakes together. And together we will meet everyone there is in this land, and we will discover the secrets of this place. And then we will decide if we want to stay or go. Does that sound like a good plan?"

"It does, Your Majesty."

"Good, then off to the kitchens!"

CHAPTER III

The Infuriating Tweedle Brothers

Later that day the new friends set off on their explorations of Wonderland, though at the time they did not yet know to call it such. The White Rabbit took the lead as he and the Queen of Hearts set down the path, neither of them knowing where it would lead them. The rabbit informed her that it was customary for servants of the crown to walk behind the monarch, but since neither of them knew if that was true, because the rabbit couldn't say how he knew such a thing, she insisted he take the lead so he could make the introductions should they encounter anyone.

The Queen was holding a small, beautifully decorated cake, and since neither she nor the rabbit knew how many of her subjects they would meet that day, or even how many there were in this land, the Queen decided it was best to have a number of her servants follow behind them in a caravan with an abundance of cakes.

Arranging for the cakes and their transport was a much easier task than delivering them. The Queen's servants were most congenial, and happy to provide the Queen with whatever she needed. The White Rabbit had wisely suggested she go straight to the kitchens by means of the servants' way so she could avoid an awkward encounter with the King, cautioning her not to mention to anyone it was her first day or ask them if they were experiencing the same phenomenon. So the Queen marched into the kitchens as if she had done so countless times before, and for all she knew, she had.

They were quite the sight, walking down the long stretch of road, looking as if they knew exactly where

The Infuriating Tweedle Brothers

they were going when in fact they did not. They walked on cobblestone paths lined with giant mushrooms and beautiful red roses, and gentle voices rose up in song from seemingly nowhere. As they passed a patch of colorful flowers, the Queen was surprised to see they had faces, and that it was the flowers themselves who sang songs that drifted on the breeze. How very strange and lovely. There was beauty everywhere she looked, from the sun streaming through the branches of tall trees to butterflies hovering as if by magic. Soon the cobblestones turned into a dirt path, the trees grew closer together, and the sunlight only found its way through in little slits. Before they knew it, they were in a dense forest.

Two strange beings stood at a crossroads, wearing suspenders and tiny pinwheel hats and making quite the spectacle. They bumped into each other over and over as they chattered away, completely oblivious to the Queen and the rabbit who were standing there looking at them. Regardless, it was a relief to see them, because they were both starting to wonder if this land had any inhabitants at all, and how could one be queen without any subjects? And since neither of them knew which road would be best to venture down next, perhaps these gentlemen would be of some assistance.

"I say, maybe these fellows will be of some help," said the rabbit. "Perhaps they know where we might find the others who live here."

"Provided there *are* others. I suppose we didn't stop to think there may not be many who live here. But . . . what do you make of these . . . uh . . . persons, Rabbit?" She spoke under her breath, careful not to get the attention of these strange beings. "Do you know who they are, Rabbit? I'm not sure if we should approach them." She was eyeing the men suspiciously, as though she was quite convinced any interaction with these two would be unpleasant.

"I don't, Your Majesty. Remember, today is my first day as well."

"They do look rather odd, don't you think? With their hats, gigantic bow ties, and high-waisted pants, it's no wonder that enormous raven is eyeing them so intently."

The Infuriating Tweedle Brothers

And it was true, there was a very large raven sitting on a sturdy branch on a tree to their left. The two small gentlemen were in the shade of the tree and didn't seem to notice the raven looking down at them as they bounced about. They didn't seem to notice anything at all but themselves. And the Queen had to wonder if this was their first day, too, even though it didn't seem so. They looked as if they had spent their lives in the same spot, having the same conversation day after day. The way they chattered and moved in sync had the practiced ease of a dance. It seemed more like a performance than an actual conversation.

"Shall we venture closer?" asked the rabbit, taking the men's measure.

"Yes, Rabbit, why don't we? As long as you think it's safe to approach."

As they took a few tentative steps, they noticed the two men were fighting over what looked to be a child's rattle. They were snatching it back and forth from each other, over and over, until it finally fell to the ground and cracked. This caused both of the men to wail, screaming so loudly the raven in the

Heartbroken

branches ruffled its feathers, and leaving the Queen and rabbit to wonder if it was wise to attempt an introduction while these men were in such a state. It seemed they should probably find a better time, though quite frankly the Queen would have been perfectly content not to meet them at all, let alone for them to be the very first of her subjects she met on her first day. And just as she thought to tell the rabbit it was best for them to try to slip away quietly, the strange brothers, for surely that is what they were, each of them looking exactly like the other in every way, started to become even more agitated than they had been before.

"Now you've done it!" cried one. "You've spoiled our rattle! I declare we have a battle!"

The Queen took a deep breath and closed her eyes, trying not to lose her patience with these odd little men. She didn't even know them. But it did seem absurd to be so incensed over a broken rattle. She almost said something to try to defuse the situation but found herself morbidly mesmerized by the imbecilic tableau unfolding in front of her.

The Infuriating Tweedle Brothers

"If you insist, dear brother. If it's a battle you want, then I shall not contradict you," said the second.

"I think we'd better just leave them to their quarrel, don't you, Rabbit? Besides, I don't like the look of that raven, you'd better stay close to me." The Queen motioned to the caravan that they would be taking a right at the crossroads, hoping they could skirt past these strange men unnoticed.

"I wouldn't go that way!" said one of the strange men suddenly. Upon closer observation, the Queen could see his name was written on the lapels of his shirt, though she wasn't sure what she should call him.

"And why is that, Mr. . . . uh . . ."

"Tweedle! We are the Tweedle brothers, and we are about to have a battle!"

"I see, then we won't keep you any longer." The Queen tried her best to move past the men, who seemingly forgot all about their battle and were now standing in her way looking quite offended, arms crossed and scowls on their faces. Based on the Queen's experience in this land thus far, she realized

Heartbroken

it was just the sort of place where two strange beings, neither of whom had paid her the slightest bit of attention at first, would suddenly decide to give her all of their attention the moment she wanted nothing more than to get away from them. She had a strong feeling that this first encounter was a portent of things to come.

"That's not proper edict! That's not polite!" said the man whose collar read *Tweedledee*. With his arms crossed, he resembled a sentinel standing at guard.

Oh, this is too much! These can't be the first subjects I meet. And if they are indeed, they certainly can't be what all subjects in this land are like, or else I shall lose my mind! This can't be happening, the Queen thought.

She looked, horror-struck, at the White Rabbit and remembered that he was one of her subjects as well, and so far he seemed to be very curious, inspiring, and rather helpful. He seemed like a wise rabbit, and possibly a very good friend. So not all was lost, even if so far, other than the rabbit, she was met with nothing but vexations.

"Excuse me, good sirs, but you are addressing

our Queen. It is not for you to tell our Queen what is proper edict or polite," scolded the White Rabbit.

I am loving this rabbit more and more.

"And how were we expected to know who she is without proper introductions? Proper introductions are proper manners. Anyone can put on a queen's dress and call themselves the Queen, but unless she is introduced as the Queen, we don't know who she is!"

Oh, this is too much. Proper manners indeed.

"I see," said the Queen. Her head spun with the number of times Tweedledee used the words *proper* and *queen*, considering she had only just learned she was the Queen today and nothing at all seemed proper in this place. Or maybe what was proper to her was not proper here. She did her best not to explode in anger, for she felt it rising within her. There was something about these men that made her want to wring their necks. Who were they, anyway, suggesting she wasn't proper? Suggesting she might not be a queen. Who were they to suggest anything at all, considering just moments ago they were about to have a war over a rattle?

Heartbroken

"I hope you're not insinuating our Queen isn't proper." It was as if she and the White Rabbit shared the same thought, and she was happy to see he was just as annoyed with these imbeciles as she was. She loved that the White Rabbit had been, up to this point, levelheaded and optimistic, but she was also happy to see this other side of him as well.

"All the other members of royalty have introduced themselves to us! The Red Queen, the White Queen, the Duchess, the White Knight, and so on! But you! You just walk past us, without a hello or how do you do? That's rude! That's not the way to start."

Tweedledum's words brought on a deluge of anger. It was surprising, really, the intensity of her hate for the Tweedle brothers considering their short acquaintance, but there it was. She detested these men.

"Rabbit, would you say it's like me to get angry? Did I get angry when I fell off the hedge?"

"No, Your Majesty, you didn't."

"And was I angry when I woke up next to a stranger in my bed?"

The Infuriating Tweedle Brothers

"I couldn't say, Your Majesty. I wasn't there, but I venture to say you were more frightened than angry."

"Correct. But you, gentlemen, and I use the word *gentlemen* lightly, have made me angry! I will not stand here to be scolded or lectured like a schoolgirl about proper edict. Exactly what did you expect of me, to stand here all day awaiting the resolution of your childish argument before I could pass?"

"We expected you to introduce yourself! That's what you're supposed to do!" said the brothers in unison, startling the Queen. How strange both of their faces looked, with their wide smiles that spread across their cruel-looking mouths as if they were about to gobble up her sweet Little Rabbit, perhaps gobble them both.

"This, my good fellows, is the Queen of Hearts," said the White Rabbit, pushing out his chest and sounding very stern and official. "Consider yourselves properly introduced!" The Queen was taken aback by the name he had chosen for her right there on the spot, but something about it resonated with her, as if she had always been the Queen of Hearts.

Heartbroken

The Queen of Hearts. My, that sounds rather nice. Oh yes, I love this rabbit.

"Then you must know the Knave of Hearts. He must be in your court." Tweedledum looked at the Queen in such a way it caused her to take a few steps back. There was something sinister in his childlike manner. She found it untrustworthy, and alarming.

"It seems you know everyone in this kingdom," she replied without missing a beat, eyeing the brothers. Her imagination went wild when she let herself look directly at their faces. Their heads were like great gourds, their mouths stretching across their expansive faces in the most disturbing way.

"And it seems you do not know anyone in this kingdom," said Tweedledum.

"It must be your first day," said Tweedledee.

"To be fair, it seems to be almost everyone's first day," said Tweedledum.

"What do you know of first days?" asked the rabbit.

"We don't know much, but we do know the story of the Mock Turtle and the Gryphon." The Tweedle brothers laughed to themselves in such a way it made

The Infuriating Tweedle Brothers

the Queen want to slap them both until they started talking sense.

"The Mock Turtle? Isn't that a soup?" The Queen wasn't sure how she knew that, but she was almost sure she had heard someone, somewhere, speak of mock turtle soup.

"No, it's a Mock Turtle. Do you know what you have in common with a Mock Turtle?" asked Tweedledum.

"I do not, Mr. Tweedle," said the Queen, maintaining her outward poise while inside she imagined screaming at the man and wringing his neck.

"You both *thought* you were one thing, and you discovered you're another." Something about his words sent terror into her soul. What did they mean? What would these inane, ill-mannered little men know of her?

"What do you mean? I demand you tell me!" She felt herself unable to hide her rage from these fools any longer. It was bubbling up in her, like a kettle on the stove. She could feel her cheeks turning red, her fists tighten.

Heartbroken

"Oh, you will see," said the Tweedle brothers in unison, laughing, and dancing, and playing leapfrog down one of the paths, quite forgetting the Queen and rabbit were there.

"Oh, this is insufferable!" she said, shaking her head.

"Indeed! Come along. There is no reason to linger," said the rabbit. But neither of them budged. The Queen and rabbit stood transfixed as the Tweedle brothers continued with their tomfoolery, causing one of them (neither she nor the rabbit, when she asked him, could be sure which of the brothers was the offender) to step on the rattle and shatter it into tiny bits.

"Now you've done it! You've spoiled our rattle! I declare we have a battle!" said the other Tweedle.

"Should we just leave the cake and make our way down the opposite road?" the rabbit whispered.

"Good idea, Rabbit. If we're lucky, they will choke on it! Or perhaps, at the very least, the next person who happens by will be spared their mindless chatter while they're eating." She laughed as if her

The Infuriating Tweedle Brothers

words were in jest, but she wondered if the rabbit could tell she was just pretending not to be entirely serious. The last thing she wanted was to make the wrong impression on her new friend, for that was what he was quickly becoming.

"Thank you for not mentioning to the Tweedles how I became angry when I told you the story of waking up next to the King."

"Well, Your Majesty, you didn't ask me if *that* made you angry, and honestly, it's none of their business."

"Too right. And, Rabbit, how did you come up with my name?"

"The Queen of Hearts? I don't know, it just seemed to fit. It seems right somehow."

"I agree, Rabbit. Thank you. And perhaps if you could be so kind to answer another question: Why are we giving the Tweedles a cake? It's like rewarding bad behavior," she asked, handing it over.

"Because we set out to deliver a cake to everyone in the kingdom, and we're not going to let the likes of them ruin our day or our dispositions, now are we?"

Heartbroken

She couldn't help but smile when the White Rabbit was so serious, and she wouldn't dare say so to his face, but she found his earnestness quite adorable.

"Indeed not, Rabbit! Let's just put it over there on the rock. Make haste, they're on their way back, and I want to be away as quickly as we can manage.

She watched the rabbit make his way to the rock near the tree where they had first spied the dreaded Tweedle brothers. She sighed and closed her eyes as their voices grew nearer, still arguing over the rattle. But even so, she was starting to feel calmer; the White Rabbit did seem to have a way of making her feel more at ease. And just as she was about to put the Tweedle debacle behind her and embolden herself to take the rabbit's advice to push forward with their adventure, she heard a loud caw and the sound of powerful wings. It was the large raven, who she had completely forgotten about until she saw it swooping down toward the White Rabbit.

"Rabbit! No! Watch out!" But it wasn't the rabbit the raven was after, and it wasn't the Tweedles, even though by the looks of terror on the Tweedle

The Infuriating Tweedle Brothers

brothers' faces they seemed quite sure the raven was about to attack them. Both brothers ran down a curious-looking path and out of sight, leaving the raven to partake in his actual quarry, and giving the Queen a respite from their arguing.

"Come along, Rabbit. Let the raven enjoy its cake. Now, which way do you think we should go?" The Queen was trying to shake off her anxiety and doing her best to find the amusement in their situation, but the truth was she was terribly afraid the raven was going to snatch the White Rabbit and take him to places unknown. Thank goodness the raven seemed to prefer cake to rabbits. This Wonderland was already proving to be a strange place, and she had only seen but a fraction of it.

"Let's go left, Your Majesty," said the rabbit rather deliberately, as if he knew for a fact that was the way they should go. She loved that about him, always seeming so sure about himself and what was the right thing to do. At least one of them did. She honestly didn't know what she would do without him. She tried to imagine what this day would be like if the

Heartbroken

White Rabbit hadn't happened upon her in the hedge maze. What would she have done? Would she have been brave enough to explore this unusual land on her own, or would she have gone back into the castle to face her stranger of a husband? She did wonder what the King was thinking, since upon waking that morning she had screamed and run out of the room. She had not heard from him since. She thought it was curious he didn't come after her, or send anyone to see if she was well. It made her think she had made the right decision to run away from a man who didn't give two figs about his wife.

"Your Majesty, did you hear me? If it's agreeable to you, I think we should go left." The rabbit's voice brought the Queen out of her musings.

"And why left, Little Rabbit? Because the Tweedles went right?"

"Left just seems like the best way to go."

"What do you think they meant, Rabbit? That business about me thinking I am one thing but finding out that I am another?"

"We all change, don't we, Your Majesty? Perhaps

The Infuriating Tweedle Brothers

that's all they meant. Besides, I'm not sure we should take them too seriously. They don't seem reliable."

"Quite right. Perhaps the next person we meet will be more levelheaded."

"I daresay they will be, and far less infuriating," said the rabbit. But the Queen could tell this time, the rabbit wasn't at all convinced he was right.

CHAPTER IV

THE CURIOUSLY RUDE CATERPILLAR

The new friends, one a queen and the other a talking rabbit, walked up a beautiful, winding garden path filled with colorful flowers as the sun started to lower in the sky. The Queen stopped and stood on the cobblestone path for a moment, taking in the splendor of the peaceful garden. She loved how the golden light blurred the vivid colors, making the landscape look as if it were painted in watercolors. She took a deep breath, happy to be out of the company of the Tweedles, and allowed herself to admire the splendors of this land she supposed was hers.

She found herself in awe of an enormous tree

The Curiously Rude Caterpillar

that was at the center of the garden, its branches stretched on either side like it was waiting for an embrace. When she and the rabbit took a closer look, they noticed a number of small, corked glass bottles tied to the tree branches with ribbon, and attached to the ribbons were little tags with the words *Drink me* written on them. This was the sort of mystery and adventure the Queen was hoping for, not being waylaid on the road by juvenile men fighting over a rattle.

"Now this is intriguing, Rabbit. What do you think? Should we?" she asked, plucking one of the bottles from the tree and holding it for him to see. She loved the way the glass bottles sparkled in the fading sunlight.

"I wouldn't advise it, my Queen. Perhaps just put one in your pocket for later." The rabbit eyed the tree suspiciously. He looked so small to her standing beneath the tree, but then again, rabbits were small creatures. Somehow she had begun to think of him as a person, and had to remind herself he was not. Nevertheless, she wished that he was bigger so they could speak eye to eye, without her constantly having to stoop down, which was uncomfortable, and would make her look smaller in stature to her subjects, should she encounter any. Never mind the fact that she found herself worrying about him being such a small rabbit in a big world.

"I think I will drink it, Rabbit! Perhaps just a sip. What will it hurt? How are we going to learn anything about this place if we don't partake? Come on, Rabbit, join me!" she said, uncorking the bottle and wiggling it before him as if she were trying to tempt him with a confection rather than a mysterious liquid they found on the side of the path.

"I don't think I will, Your Majesty, but thank you all the same."

"Very well, Rabbit!" she said, taking a sip. "It's quite tasty, you should have some." She took another sip and hiccupped rather violently, causing her entire body to jolt.

"Rabbit! What's happened? It looks as if you are growing larger in size!" As she watched her friend grow taller, she wondered if she had acquired some

The Curiously Rude Caterpillar

magical wish-granting power, because she had just wished they were closer in size.

"No, my Queen, it's not I who have grown, but you who have shrunk." He eyed her with quite a peculiar expression.

"I think you're right, Rabbit!"

Everything around her was enormous. The tree, which was already quite large, seemed impossibly high, and suddenly she realized what it was like to be smaller than a rabbit. She made a silent promise that she must always protect her new little friend.

"Well, this is an interesting development." She wondered if she didn't prefer to be this size, as just moments before she wanted them to be the same size and now they were. It pleased her more than she thought it might.

"Indeed it is, Your Majesty. Perhaps we should look for something to make you tall again?"

"We shall see, Rabbit, we shall see. I think I like being small. It is quite nice to speak with you eye to eye," she said, smiling. "Besides, if I weren't small, then I wouldn't be able to venture into that little cave and see what is causing that curious smoke. See there?" She pointed to an overgrown area the Queen would never have been able to go through if she hadn't drunk the contents of the bottle she had, just by chance, found hanging on a tree right outside this mysterious cave.

"I think this is all by design, Rabbit," she said with a mischievous grin as she took to the path, motioning for the rabbit to follow her. "Come on! Let's see what is in there!"

"But what about the servants?"

"Tell them to wait!"

She was far too excited to wait herself and rushed off, leaving the rabbit to deal with the servants. He caught up with her, out of breath, a few moments later.

The inside of the cave was dark and smelled strongly of incense. It took a few seconds for her eyes to adjust, and when they did, the Queen blinked.

Though nothing about this day had been what she would consider normal, she still was not prepared to find a peculiarly large caterpillar sitting upon a particularly tall mushroom. It took her several moments

The Curiously Rude Caterpillar

to remember that it was not the Caterpillar but the Queen who was of a peculiar size. The Caterpillar was quite ordinary, except for the fact that he was smoking a pipe, which she presumed was the source of the smoke.

The Caterpillar took no notice of the peculiar-size queen or the rabbit. His back was to them as he took long puffs from his pipe and blew out the smoke in a wild dance of long tendrils, curlicues, and circles. The rabbit cleared his throat in an attempt to get the Caterpillar's attention, but when he turned to see what the noise might be, he didn't see them standing beneath the tall mushroom and promptly went back to what he was doing.

This is intolerable. Dancing men in schoolboy clothes, shrinking potions, and now I'm being ignored by a smoking caterpillar. This is too much, thought the Queen, but she didn't share her thoughts aloud, and certainly not with the rabbit. She had lost her temper far too many times already that day, and she didn't want to be a tiresome person who did nothing but complain.

She reminded herself that this might not be *too*

much at all, and in fact could be considered more than tolerable. She had no basis for comparison. For all she knew, this was the way things were, though a voice inside told her it was not. Nevertheless, she decided the best thing to do was climb upon a smaller mushroom so she could get the Caterpillar's attention. Perhaps she wasn't giving him a chance. For all she knew, he was perfectly polite and would speak to her once he saw her, and then she would feel foolish for assuming he was being rude to her intentionally. So even though she hadn't had much luck with climbing things that day, she saw no other course of action but to climb onto a mushroom so she could speak with a caterpillar that was three times her size. Normal, indeed.

Once she had a better view of the creature, she found herself rather mesmerized as he sang an unusual song in a rather condescending tone—not to mention his antennae—even though he had a strangely human face, and protruding lips that produced large purple smoke rings. Admittedly, she should have introduced herself immediately, especially after all the hoopla she had gone through with the Tweedle brothers, but she just stood there staring at the insect. She would think she had never considered insects to be of much consequence before that day except the truth was she didn't know if she had ever considered such things.

"WHO . . . ARE . . . YOU?" the Caterpillar asked, startling her. Puffs of smoke drifted from his mouth, up and out of sight.

The Queen didn't know how to answer because she didn't really know who she was. She decided this time she would take the rabbit's advice and not admit to anyone this was her first day, but before she could answer, her sweet, furry friend chimed in.

"This, sir, is the Queen of Hearts," came the White Rabbit's voice from below. He was standing just under the Queen's mushroom, doing his very best to project his voice. She had to admit that despite the circumstances he sounded rather official, which in turn made the Queen feel official. It was funny, she had almost forgotten she wasn't just on an adventure with her friend, but she was the Queen, and this was her first outing in an official capacity to meet all of her subjects. Leave it to the rabbit to keep her on track.

"IS . . . THAT . . . RIGHT?" The supercilious caterpillar narrowed his eyes, as if inspecting her. It was rather laughable, really, the idea of a queen being sized up by a caterpillar. She could tell immediately he knew nothing of manners and seemed to think very highly of himself. He wasn't really in the position to size anyone up, no matter what his own size might be.

"It is. Now, won't you introduce yourself to me?" The Queen was doing her best to be patient, though she was quickly learning that was not one of her virtues—at least not in this world.

"WHY?" he asked in the same pompous tone, and she wondered why she was wasting her time talking to a caterpillar in the first place. And then she just started to laugh, she couldn't help it, as the lunacy of the situation suddenly hit her. Never mind she was talking to a caterpillar, but she was talking to a disagreeable caterpillar at that. And she wondered something for the first time since she had woken up

The Curiously Rude Caterpillar

that morning: Could this, perhaps, be all a dream? What if this was just an outlandish, peculiar, and vexing dream, and at any moment she was going to wake up and realize none of it was real? But how could she possibly know if this was a dream or not? It wasn't as if she knew what was usual or unusual. Perhaps it was completely ordinary to wake up and not remember who you were and try to get answers from an imperious caterpillar, the thought of which made her laugh again, even louder, because it seemed to the Queen the Caterpillar acted more like royalty than she did. But then again, how would she know what royalty acted like?

"Oh dear. Why does everything have to be so confusing in this place?" The Queen didn't mean to say that aloud, but it wasn't as if she could take it back now. Perhaps this high-handed creature had an answer.

"It doesn't have to be," said the Caterpillar snobbishly.

"Well, it has been for me," she said, wondering why she was sharing this with someone who seemed to care very little for anyone but himself. But perhaps she wasn't giving this smug caterpillar a chance. Maybe if she talked to him long enough he would have some wisdom to share. Or maybe, as her instincts were telling her, she would end up wanting to wring his neck.

"WHY?"

Was there anything this damnable Caterpillar said besides why?

She was about to lose her temper.

"Why is it so confusing? Well, to start with, I can't remember things as I used to. Or at least, I don't think I can."

"Then, I ask again, WHO . . . ARE . . . YOU?"

She wanted to scream *I DON'T KNOW!* because, really, she didn't. She was angry with herself that she had gone against the rabbit's advice when she had resigned herself to take it. The Caterpillar must have known she didn't know who she was, elsewise he wouldn't keep asking. But she didn't know how to respond.

As she stood there in bewilderment in a cloud

The Curiously Rude Caterpillar

of pink smoke, she decided the best thing to do was offer the creature the cake she had brought him and then take her leave of him.

"Rabbit, we seem to have forgotten the Caterpillar's cake. Will you go fetch it for me, please? And then I think we should set off on our way."

"What would I want with a cake?" asked the Caterpillar arrogantly, pushing her to the edge of explosive anger, or at least it seemed so to the Queen.

"Well, I don't know. Perhaps to eat it?" She said it with sarcasm, even as she wondered the same thing herself.

"It doesn't seem like you know much of anything," said the rude insect.

"Then I shall take my leave, Caterpillar. Good day!" And with that, she jumped down from the mushroom and stomped her way out of the Caterpillar's lair. She was outside before she remembered she had left the rabbit behind, and, besides that, he hadn't yet gone to fetch the cake. She paused, wondering what to do next.

"You there, come back. I have something

important to say." The Caterpillar's voice wafted out of the cave in a puff of smoke. She sighed. She hadn't intended to look back, but for the first time the Caterpillar's voice sounded earnest. She turned on her heel and ducked back inside.

"Well," she asked impatiently. "What is it?"

"Keep your temper."

"Keep my *what*?"

"Your temper. And if you're going to be queen, might I suggest you grow a bit taller?"

"Taller? Taller than what?"

"Taller than you are. You're rather small for a queen, aren't you?"

"Am I? I thought you were rather large for a caterpillar." She thought for a moment. "I am rather small from drinking that potion, aren't I? How could I have forgotten?"

"That was by design."

"I thought it might be. But how am I to tell who is meant to be small and who is not with all these potions just hanging about for the drinking? For all I know you are a giant caterpillar, and I am the correct size."

The Curiously Rude Caterpillar

"I guess it depends on perspective. It's been my impression that humans, especially kings and queens, like to be bigger than those who serve them."

"And what about Rabbit there?" she asked, gesturing to her furry white friend, who had caught up to her and now stood at her side. "Would you say he is the size of an average rabbit? I think we could both do with growing a bit larger."

"What do you know of the average size of rabbits, or even the average size of anyone? Today is your first day. For all you know, you started out small and just thought you shrunk." The Caterpillar gave her a knowing look.

"But you just said the shrinking was by design."

"Hmm. Did I?"

"You can't trick me! Besides, my queendom didn't seem particularly large when I awoke. If I had already been the size of a caterpillar, wouldn't everything have been far larger? Oh, this doesn't make any sense. I think you're trying to confuse me."

"Am I?"

"I think you are, and I have no idea why!"

Heartbroken

"I am just telling you the truth. I am sorry if you don't want to hear it."

"I have no evidence that anyone here except for Rabbit tells the truth." As she spoke, she wondered if there even was such a thing as truth in a place like this.

"Your Majesty, I assure you, the potion you drank just moments ago did indeed make you smaller," said the rabbit.

"Too right. Thank you, Rabbit. Now, please, Mr. Caterpillar, won't you tell me how to grow larger again? As you so aptly pointed out, queens like to be larger than their subjects. While I think it might be fun to be small, eventually I will need to return to my castle, and when I do, I should much prefer not to sleep in a mouse hole or a doll's house." The Queen wondered if that might be preferable to sleeping next to a stranger, though she did not say so aloud.

"Everyone knows," said the Caterpillar, "that mice live in teapots."

"Teapots? What kind of mouse lives in a teapot?"

"The Dormouse!"

The Curiously Rude Caterpillar

"The *door mouse*? Whyever is he called that when he lives in a teapot?"

"Teapot Mouse is an absurd name. Please, show some common sense." The Caterpillar seemed to enjoy the Queen's confusion.

"But you are being nonsensical!" the Queen cried. She was well past trying to hide her anger. She felt it bubbling inside her, growing larger and filling up her body, making her heart race and her head spin. There was no way she was going to be able to keep this inside, and it would all explode into rage, or tears. She feared if she did begin to cry she wouldn't ever be able to stop, and so rage was the far more appealing of the two. She felt her face turning red with anger.

"HOLD . . . YOUR . . . TEMPER!" the Caterpillar said sternly, blowing a puff of smoke in her direction.

"I will not hold my temper! And I will not take orders from a pompous, supercilious, self-important, overblown, puffed-up, butterfly larva!"

"And I will not take a cake from a diminutive hotheaded queen!"

"Then you shall have no cake! Rabbit, I think it's

Heartbroken

time we take our cake elsewhere!" She turned to leave, then looked back one last time, her rage exploding. "And for the record, it is *you*, sir, who is absurd! You *and* this place. I am done here. Rabbit, come along!" And with that, she rushed off.

But once the Queen got back to her servants it was *she* who felt absurd, standing there so much smaller than everyone. She realized the Caterpillar was right: queens do not like being smaller than their subjects. And just as she was about to complain about their latest encounter, she realized the rabbit hadn't followed her back to the path where the servants were waiting for them.

"Rabbit! Where are you? Rabbit?" she called out, but before she truly began to panic she saw his white ears emerge from the bushes.

"Thank goodness you're okay, Rabbit! That was outrageous! Remind me never again to speak to caterpillars who don't even have the decency to turn into butterflies."

"Well, he did give me something to pass along to you, Your Majesty. It's a piece of his mushroom," he said with a sly smile as he showed it to her.

"Disgusting! What would I want with a piece of his dirty mushroom? Is this place getting to you, Rabbit? Are you quite all right, trying to give me a disgusting mushroom as if it's a rare gem?"

"Your Majesty, please, you will like this mushroom, I assure you. Apparently, if you eat it, you will grow large again."

"I see. Well, thank you, Rabbit. You are proving yourself most helpful. I daresay this excursion has been very unproductive. The only helpful creature we've met was a giant raven. But come to think of it, we didn't actually get to meet it, did we?"

"Though it did seem to enjoy the cake, so there is that, Your Majesty!"

"There is that, Little Rabbit. So, where do we go next?"

"Are you sure you want to keep going? It is getting dark, and we might want to think about getting back to the castle, if you don't mind the suggestion."

"I want you to always feel like you may make suggestions, Rabbit, but that doesn't guarantee I will

Heartbroken

take them. I say we venture forth, but first maybe a bite of that mushroom. How much do you think it will take to get back to my original size?"

"I don't think *original* size factors in, considering we don't know anything other than today."

"True. Why don't we both take a bite and see what happens?"

"Me, Your Majesty?" The Queen thought the rabbit looked adorable with his little paw pressed to his chest, his eyes full of wonder that she should suggest he, too, should take a bite.

"Why not? Wouldn't you like to be bigger? I quite like us being the same size."

"Why not, indeed!" said the rabbit, and they each took a bite.

"Oh no! This will not do," said the Queen, realizing they were now looking down upon the treetops of the forest. "I wish these pesky clouds weren't in our way, else we might be able to see the entire kingdom from up here."

"Indeed, Your Majesty. I think we ate too much!"

"Oh, this is far too large, Rabbit! What do we

The Curiously Rude Caterpillar

do?" said the Queen, wondering what the servants thought of them now, towering over them. Were they afraid? She didn't know, she couldn't see them from such a height. The rabbit bent down and plucked a bottle for each of them off the tree with a giant paw.

"Here, take a sip of this!" he said, producing the bottle of shrinking potion for the Queen, keeping one for himself.

"I wouldn't dare! I don't want to be small again. Oh, this is the worst day I have ever had!"

"So far as you know, it's the only day you've ever had!" said the rabbit. "Come on, Your Majesty, let's just take the tiniest of sips until we are the right size. What do you say?"

"And how do we know what size is the right size?"

"I suspect we will know it when it happens."

The Queen took the cork out of the bottle and took a tiny sip, which instantly made her shrink down a few feet. She looked up at the White Rabbit, who was now towering over her.

"How does it feel to be taller than everyone, Rabbit?" she called up to him. She had to admit he looked rather impressive from this vantage, though it would not do at all for him to stay larger than her, of course.

"Rather peculiar, but not at all disagreeable, my Queen!" he said, laughing. "I feel quite important."

"Yes, well, that's enough of that, then. Come down now, please." The rabbit held the tiny bottle to his large muzzle and took a small sip. Within seconds, he had shrunk down to her size.

"Ah, there you are! Yes. Will this do, then, Rabbit? Would you say we are the right size now?" asked the Queen.

"I think not, Your Majesty. See!" He pointed down to the servants, who were still considerably smaller. Or depending on one's point of view, the Queen and the rabbit were still considerably taller.

"Too right. One more sip, perhaps a slightly bigger one this time? Ready?" asked the Queen.

"Ready!" said the rabbit. They both took another sip, and with a jolt they shrunk again.

"This seems about right," said the Queen, comparing her height to her servants, who still looked much smaller than her, or, considering from their perspective, it was she who looked much larger than them.

"Does it seem right, my Queen? You and I are the same size."

"As I already said, I quite like us being the same size, Rabbit. And besides, your pocket watch is now proportionate. Though we will have to get you another bumbershoot. And while it's true I am a bit larger than I was, I think I quite like the idea of being much taller than the King," she said.

"Do you think he will mind?" asked the rabbit.

"I have no idea what he will or won't mind, Rabbit. I don't know him. At least, I don't think I do. But let's keep the rest of that mushroom and some of those potions in case we need them again. And let's keep it between us," she said, smiling at the rabbit.

"Well, between us and the servants," the rabbit replied. But when the rabbit and Queen turned their gazes from each other, they found that the servants were gone.

"Rabbit! Where did they go? They were just here!

Heartbroken

How could they be gone in a flash like that?" The Queen looked in every direction trying to catch sight of them. "Do you see any tracks? This is outrageous! Why would they have left like that, without a word?"

"Or a 'by your leave'!"

"By my what?"

"Your leave, Your Majesty. They are not allowed to leave without your permission."

"That's true!" the Queen said, and it began to dawn on her that she had quite a lot of power. "I did not give them permission to leave! This is very strange, Rabbit. How could we lose an entire group of servants in the blink of an eye? Do you think there is magic in these lands?"

"Well, it does have potions to make you shrink and mushrooms that make you grow, so it wouldn't be unreasonable to think so."

"True. Well, we have to find them, Rabbit. And we have to be careful."

"Look, Your Majesty, I think they went this way." The rabbit bent to the ground, his nose twitching. "This looks like their tracks, does it not? And look,

The Curiously Rude Caterpillar

here are impressions made by the wheels of a cart, leading down that path."

The Queen's gaze followed the path into a dark brambly wood.

"But this is curious, don't you think, Rabbit? What would cause them to go in there? It does look rather foreboding, doesn't it? I mean, really, who goes wandering into a dark forest right as the sun is going down? And how did they manage to slip away so quickly without us noticing?"

"I suppose we weren't paying attention, Your Majesty. Perhaps they were afraid of all our growing and shrinking. We were rather occupied by our height dilemma. Our heads were in the clouds, one might say."

"Indeed so, Rabbit! We'd better see what happened to them."

"Should we follow the path, then? Didn't those Tweedles say this was exactly the direction we should avoid?" The rabbit looked a bit nervous.

"Did they? I don't recall. Look, Rabbit, the last thing I want to do is go into this dark forest, but I don't see a way around it. I have a duty to my servants, even if they are too dimwitted not to wander into places unknown."

"Isn't that exactly what we decided to do today when we set off on this adventure? Venture into places unknown?"

"While I agree, I must point out there is a difference between a sensible adventure and traipsing off into a dark, scary-looking forest right as the sun is going down. I think we both have more sense than that. But there is nothing for it, we have to go after them. Just think of what might befall them if we abandon them to this dreadful place!"

"I can't imagine anything more dreadful than the Caterpillar," said the rabbit. The Queen loved it when he said such things. It made her laugh because it sounded like something she would say. If anything about this day was a success, it was befriending the White Rabbit.

"You sound as annoyed as I am, Rabbit. I'll tell you, I am not at all impressed with this place so far, not in the least."

"Except for the shrinking and growing."

The Curiously Rude Caterpillar

"Yes, that was fun," she said, laughing. "Perhaps there is more fun to be had."

"I doubt we will find it in that forest," said the rabbit, pointing to a sign that read:

TULGEY WOOD

"What does it mean, Rabbit?"

"I don't know, but if I were venture to guess, I would say it means dark and foreboding."

"Oh, Rabbit, muster up some courage! We're off to the woods to save our friends!"

"Your servants, Your Majesty. Not your friends."

"Yes, yes, Rabbit. You are always right."

"May I quote you on that, Your Majesty?"

"Best not to, Rabbit. You know how queens can be. Or maybe you don't, I certainly don't, having just become one. But I'm sure you can imagine."

"I do hope you won't be one of those queens who throw their subjects in the dungeon or chop off their heads over the slightest offense."

"Don't be silly, Rabbit," the Queen said, marching confidently into Tulgey Wood. "If I chop off someone's head, you can be sure I will have a good reason."

Chapter V

From the Book of Fairy Tales

The Light in the Dead Woods

The Dead Woods would be unrecognizable to the old queens who once ruled there, should they decide to rise from their slumber and walk among the dead once more. They would see its vast cemeteries and grounds were now entirely covered in golden flowers and be horrified that the new witch queens of the Dead Woods, Circe, Primrose, and Hazel, did not hoard the flowers away like their predecessors but shared them with everyone in the Many Kingdoms. They would find that even the weeping angels who stood silent and beautiful at the many tombs and crypts looked more at peace, not tormented by grief but weeping for joy, now that their kingdom was filled with love and light.

The one thing the Dead Woods did hoard, however, was the dead. For more years than anyone could now properly recollect, the many Queens of the Dead throughout the ages demanded the neighboring villages bring their dead to be buried or interred in their kingdom. Failing to do so would mean death to everyone in that village. Circe, Primrose, and Hazel did away with this nightmarish practice when they took their places as queens. Now the neighboring villages and kingdoms were free to bury their own dead, to build cemeteries of their own, and visit their departed loved ones as they wished. Though sometimes, even though it was widely known there was no longer a punishment for failing to do so, mourners would still bring their dead to Sir Jacob, who had been serving the Dead Woods for many generations.

Welcoming the dead was one of the many duties Sir Jacob performed for the queens of the Dead Woods throughout his years of service. Though it happened far less frequently than it had in the past, he still met mourners at the thorn-covered rosebush hedge that encircled their kingdom and ushered their unwanted dead through the red swirling vortex that only the deceased could enter. It was a melancholy task, taking the dead from these so-called mourners, like castoffs, or unwanted rubbish. And he wondered what sort of people these dead were in life that their family or friends did not want the trouble of giving them a peaceful place to rest.

This weighed heavily on Jacob's mind as he stood in the morning room waiting for Circe, Primrose, and Hazel to join him so they could discuss their preparations. The room was a massive solarium at the top of the old mansion built in the age of Queen Gothel for her adopted sisters, Primrose and Hazel. Jacob often wept for Gothel, and the previous Queens of the Dead, for everything they suffered, secretly wondering if succumbing to their hereditary delirium was their fate. When Circe, Primrose, and Hazel came into power, it was the first time he wasn't afraid. And for the first time, he saw a glimmer of light in the Dead Woods.

From the Book of Fairy Tales

Perhaps that was why it shook his very being when Circe asked him to raise their undead army and ready them for war. He felt in his core this was not the right path for their kingdom, and he feared it might undo everything the Ladies of Light had been trying to achieve since they took this mantle.

It was not in Primrose's and Hazel's nature to unleash their army of the dead on another kingdom, but he feared it might be in Circe's, even if this was an aspect of her being she did everything within her power to repress. Jacob believed in Circe's inherent goodness—she was magically created, after all, with the best parts of his daughters, Lucinda, Ruby, and Martha, causing them to go mad. Without those elements of good, all that was left was bloodthirsty madness. And he had to wonder where that mania had gone when Hades gave them peace and brought them to the Underworld. Was it flung into an abyss, or did it now reside in someone else?

Lasting happiness was something Jacob never thought possible for his daughters, and it eased his heart that they were now finally free of their madness, rage, and bloodlust, spending their afterlife most deliciously with Hades. He could hear his daughters now from the other room, talking with Circe through their magic mirrors discussing this war of Tulip's and Circe's fears if it should come to fruition. Jacob had already shared these fears with his granddaughter, and his mind was heavy with worry. He wanted to council Circe the way a grandsire might, the way he felt obliged to do not only as father to Circe's mothers but also as the most trusted and loyal servant of the crown, to advise her not to partake in this war. But he feared what he might find behind her eyes when they spoke, and he dreaded what he might have to do should he find his daughters' madness now living within his granddaughter.

Just then, as if he had summoned her, Circe walked into the room. The light that always seemed to shine from within Circe was diminished. He could see she was burdened by this upcoming war, and he was hesitant to burden her any further by sharing his misgivings.

"I know you've wanted to speak with me, Grandsire

Jacob. I'm sorry you didn't feel like you could come to me before now."

"I should have known you already knew my thoughts, little one. Even after all these years living among witches, I still sometimes forget you can read minds."

"I can also read your heart." Circe's smile was weak, and it made Jacob wonder if there was more than this impending war wearying Circe's own heart. He knew she was worried about Snow White, as the two of them were very close. Everyone in the Dead Woods had come to love Snow White, and how could they not? She was the kindest person Jacob had ever known. It was because of Snow's kindness Jacob was no longer ashamed of his appearance.

Snow White was a frequent visitor to the Dead Woods, and had only just left their company shortly before Hades's visit, when he shared his story from the Book of Fairy Tales. But soon after they were besieged by chaos, blood, and misery when the Odd Sisters arrived, ravaged by their grief, suffering, and unbearable madness. If Hades had not stepped in and spirited them away to the Underworld, Jacob shuddered to think what fresh terrors might have befallen them that terrible night. Jacob never thought happiness was possible for his daughters, but that was what Hades gave them when he took from them their madness and made them whole again, and for that, Jacob would feel forever grateful to the lord of the Underworld.

Jacob smiled despite his anxiety, remembering the night Hades had given him the outfit he was now wearing. He felt smart with his top hat, morning coat, and handsome walking cane. And though Jacob was not endowed with the power to read the thoughts of others, he had learned how to read the faces of his queens over the years and he could see Circe was afraid Snow's pleas for help were getting lost in their preparations for Tulip's war.

"I'm worried, granddaughter," he said, truly meeting her gaze for the first time since she walked into the room.

Circe put her hand on Jacob's face and held it there tenderly, just looking into his eyes. Seeing the sadness and worry in Circe's face made Jacob want to weep, and he wished he could spare her from her burdens. Circe's hand felt cold and smooth on his face, almost like marble. All of his queens had felt this way over the years, otherworldly, as if they were slowly turning into marble visages to be preserved in catacombs under the Dead Woods. He remembered the story Hades had shared with them, about how he discovered the catacombs under the Forbidden Mountain were connected to the catacombs under the Dead Woods, as well as to his realm in the Underworld. It made Jacob wonder if he shouldn't explore the catacombs himself, to see where else they might lead.

"I share your fears, Grandsire Jacob. I don't want this war with the Beast Prince and Queen Belle, but I cannot persuade Tulip to come here so we can discuss her reasons."

"I'd say her reasons are very well-known. As ancient as those reasons may be."

"Not so very ancient, all things considered. Not for those like us. Oh, Grandsire, there was a time when I would have gleefully destroyed the Beast

Prince without a word from Tulip. But as grievous as his crimes were, I cannot condone attacking his kingdom and everyone who lives under his protection. Tulip is not seeing sense, and I fear there is something sinister at work here, something we are not seeing. There is more to this than we are being told."

"Do you think Tulip is trying to deceive you?"

"No, but I have a feeling someone is deceiving her."

"Not your mothers?"

"No, not this time. And before you ask, I don't want to ask them for help. I still can't bring myself to trust them. I have to deal with this on my own."

"But you're not on your own. You have Primrose, Hazel, and me."

"I know. But I have been fearing what will happen if the three queens of the Dead Woods combine their powers to see everything at once. Look what happened to my mothers, what happened to the Queens of the Dead before them. When we first took the throne, Hazel, Primrose, and I split time, and therefore the responsibilities of those timelines between us quite unconsciously, without even meaning to. But we decided it was for the best. It was safest."

"I think that is very wise." Jacob felt a sense of relief that was still their plan. The last thing he wanted was this burden to destroy another queen of the Dead Woods.

"I think it's a wise plan, too," Circe said. "But you know how time really works—trying to break it up makes it harder to see things as my mothers do. Well, as Lucinda sees it, at any rate."

"You're right. Ruby and Martha seem to have other . . . interests." He laughed. "So what will you do?"

"I don't know. I need time to think. But there seems to be no time for even that. Before Tulip's call, Snow asked for our help. Are we to ignore her plea just because Tulip wants to war against the Beast Prince for something he did so long ago the story is almost forgotten?"

"Surely he is the King now, Circe, and Belle is his queen."

"Indeed." She eyed him, and Jacob knew she could

sense he was trying to shield his thoughts from her.

"What is it, Jacob?" she asked gently. "I know you're keeping something from me."

"I was worried your mothers' madness now resided in you, but I see you are not eager to fight this war of Tulip's, and you are taking every consideration within your power to keep yourself from going down their path."

"When I look into the mirror I don't see them behind my eyes, Grandsire. But I check every day to make sure that is still the case."

"There is one other matter I was trying to avoid bringing to your attention, but I'm afraid I cannot. It's the Red Queen's Jabberwock. It's a huge dragon under her control, at least it was when she resided in the Many Kingdoms many years ago. But it's gone missing. I have not been able to find it."

"I have never heard of this Red Queen, nor her creature."

"It's time you read the Book of Fairy Tales in its entirety, granddaughter. The Red Queen is among many who were banished from the Dead Woods long

From the Book of Fairy Tales

ago, but the Red Queen's creature, the Jabberwock, remained here in the Dead Woods, in stone form. I only took notice of its absence while gathering the other stone creatures for our forces."

"Why have I never heard of this creature or his queen? Who was she to us? Why was she banished?"

"There have been many who once lived in the Dead Woods who were banished to other worlds," said a new voice. Jacob and Circe turned to see Hazel and Primrose walking into the room. Jacob smiled to see them. He loved being in the company of all three of them. His witches. His queens. All so very different from each other, but with the same purpose. "I don't know this Red Queen's story as well as some of the others," Hazel continued, "but I bet we can find it in our library." Hazel was wearing her customary light gray, it was almost the color of tarnished silver. Jacob had always felt Hazel had a ghostly quality to her, drifting throughout the Dead Woods like a specter, while her sister Primrose bounded through it with vibrance enough for them both.

"As for the Jabberwock," Primrose added, "Hazel

and I saw it every day of our childhood, guarding the densest part of the woods." Primrose's sweet smile caused the dimples in her cheeks to appear. She looked lovely in her velvet dress, the color of fall leaves, with a wreath of red and orange flowers on her head.

"But where can this Jabberwock be?" asked Circe. "Do you think the Red Queen returned to reclaim her creature? Is this queen of our lineage? Is it possible she snuck into the Dead Woods in the dark of night and brought it to life?" asked Circe.

"Nothing so sinister as that. I think he's been missing since the Odd Sisters brought all the stone creatures to life, when they attacked the Dead Woods, causing you to send them to the Place Between. But unlike the other stone creatures, the Jabberwock never returned."

"Surely if this monster was terrorizing the Many Kingdoms we would have heard," said Circe.

"I don't think the Jabberwock is still in this world," said Primrose.

From the Book of Fairy Tales

"Not London, or Neverland?" asked Circe.

"Wherever it is, the Red Queen would be nearby," said Jacob. Circe turned to him.

"Jacob, send a raven to Tulip and inform her I have other duties to attend to before I join her. If this dragon is terrorizing another land, then it is our duty to secure the creature and bring it back here."

"But Tulip is expecting our army."

"And she will have it. Grandsire Jacob, you are more than capable of leading our army in aid of Tulip. And I know I can trust you to do what is right. I still hold out hope Tulip will see sense, or I will discover what is driving her toward this perilous path. But before I join you there, I need to find this Jabberwock, and help Snow."

"Circe, why are you suddenly so concerned with this Jabberwock? Surely Snow and Tulip are our priorities just now," said Hazel.

"And they are, but there is something nagging at me, telling me this creature plays a part in things to come. I'm sure you've felt it, this unsettling shift, this feeling as if we are standing on the edge of things."

"I have felt it," said Primrose. "And I think your mothers know what's behind it."

"I do as well," said Circe. "There are reasons beyond the Jabberwock that compel me to visit my mothers, which have not yet revealed themselves to me."

"Oh! I remember a poem in the Book of Fairy Tales about the Jabberwock. Hold on, let me see if I can find it." Primrose rushed to the bookshelf in excitement and pulled the Book of Fairy Tales down from the shelf.

"See, here it is. It says the Jabberwock lives in a place called Tulgey Wood. It's a silly sort of place with odd-looking birds . . . but wait. This is strange, this section looks new, but it's still in the Odd Sisters' voice." Primrose's brow creased in puzzlement.

"What do you mean? What's wrong?" asked Circe.

"I don't know. I guess I thought since we were the ladies of the Dead Woods, any new chapters would be in our voices. That *we* would be writing the stories."

"That would require us to combine our powers,

and I am not sure we are ready for that. I'm afraid of what might happen," said Circe.

"So we let the Odd Sisters continue to decide the fate of the Many Kingdoms?" asked Hazel, chiming in.

"I'm trying to save us from turning out like them. I need time to research, to know what we're really getting into, and to truly understand what my mothers' deaths mean for the magic they did when they were alive," said Circe.

"I thought we were going to change things, Circe. Look what we did with James. We may not have been able to save him from his fate, but we did change his timeline, if only a little. Imagine what we could do if we really tried! And what about righting the wrong with Lady Tremaine? Are we really going to let her remain in stone form after everything she went through? And what about Snow White's mirrors? She said she can hear Grimhilde's endless cries from every mirror in her castle. And how long before Aurora sends us a message saying she remembers everything that happened in the Chamber of Mirrors or she suddenly has dragon powers like her mother? There is something going on, and I guarantee it is connected to the Odd Sisters," said Hazel.

"Do you honestly believe they're causing all this from the Underworld? I don't think so, my lady," said Jacob.

"No, I don't think that's what Hazel is saying, Grandsire. But I agree it is somehow connected. Listen, I know we had a plan, and that's truly how I imagined spending our days, rewriting the Book of Fairy Tales, fixing what we could, but Tulip has turned everything upside down, and I fear somehow this Jabberwock is connected."

"How do you know?" asked Primrose.

"I don't, not for sure. Like I said, it's just a feeling. But I fear we are all in danger. And I think I need to swallow my pride and pay a visit to my mothers in the Underworld before I go to Snow's kingdom."

"Oh! You're just going to pop in to the Underworld and have a chat with your mothers, are you?" asked Primrose.

"I think I have to. I have a feeling they know far more than they're letting on."

Chapter VI

Tulgey Wood

Every dark forest has its secrets. Some are home to the dead, while others are filled with menacing leafless trees with grasping branches and eyes that glow in the darkness.

And some, like Tulgey Wood, hide unexpected and deadly creatures lurking in the shadows.

It seemed unlikely Wonderland would have such a forest, but then again, how are we to know what Wonderland should or shouldn't have within its vast and confounding borders? Because it would seem not even those who dwelled within Wonderland knew what to expect on any given day or night.

Heartbroken

Tulgey Wood seemed, at the onset, to be a rather silly place; its colorful trees and strange birds seemed to spring from the wild imagination of a child. Any adventurer might feel discombobulated by the misleading signs pointing this way and that, with conflicting bits of advice. It might even lull them into a sense of agitated whimsy, but they would never expect to feel fear. That is, unless they were afraid of birds with umbrella bodies or shovels for faces, or accordions with owl heads, or frogs in the shapes of drums.

These trifling things did not frighten the Queen of Hearts or the White Rabbit. They were almost expected, though nevertheless baffling, after everything else they had seen that day.

"I've had enough nonsense, Rabbit! This is intolerable!" said the Queen as they stood in a nexus of intertwining paths leading every which way with no indication where they should go next. "Now, Rabbit, if you were a servant, which way would you go? This way?"

"I am a servant, Your Majesty."

"Are you, Rabbit?"

Tulgey Wood

"Indeed, Your Majesty. But I have no idea where the other servants might have gone."

"Listen, Rabbit, do you hear that? It sounds like . . . voices?" The Queen quickly traversed the stream by skipping across stones protruding from the water. Once on the other side, she could hear the voices more distinctly and popped her head through a little clearing between some trees. She expected to see the servants down below.

"Rabbit, be careful!" she called out, watching him hop across the stones to meet her. "Look at this!"

They both stood in awe as they watched what looked like umbrella birds frolicking under a waterfall, flitting about and squawking as if it were the most usual thing to do, when it seemed to both the Queen and the rabbit to be rather unusual, though what did they know? This was, after all, their first day.

"Excuse me, could one of you tell me if you've seen a group of servants? I seem to have lost them."

The birds, looking rather annoyed to have their frivolities disrupted, started squawking more loudly in a rather agitated manner as they took flight, then landed on a nearby branch and glared at them.

"Rabbit! Is it just me or is everything we've encountered so far either confusing, annoying, or both? I mean, really, twins speaking in riddles, an imperious caterpillar, and now this? How was I to know these bumbershoot birds don't know how to talk?"

"I'd say they're both annoying and confusing. But perhaps it's only so because it's our first day," said the rabbit, examining the signs on a tall red tree that pointed in various directions. It was a strange sort of tree, the likes of which neither of them had ever seen. One might think the most remarkable and defining feature would be that it was red, but that wasn't it. The tree's most remarkable feature, which was universally agreed upon because almost everyone who had seen this tree had in fact remarked upon it, was that it had a series of confounding signs that were of absolutely no help to anyone venturing into the woods.

"There is wisdom in that, Rabbit, to be sure, but I have the strangest feeling I would find this place confusing and vexing no matter what day it was."

"Perhaps we should turn back, Your Majesty, lest we get lost in these woods. Like everything else we've encountered so far, these signs don't make sense, and it is getting dreadfully dark. We can send the Queen's guard to search for the servants." The Queen appreciated that the rabbit was trying to make sense of the nonsense.

"We don't even know if I have a queen's guard, Rabbit. If I do, I haven't met them yet. You'd think the King would have sent them after me, at the very least to see if I was well. No, Rabbit, I think we are on our own. Don't worry, I will protect you." She walked up behind him and took him by the paw.

"Look there, Rabbit! I can see the servants' tracks. I think we should go this way," she said, pointing to where footprints led down the path. She followed them, then bumped into what she thought was a birdcage hanging on a low branch.

"Oh! Excuse me," she said, realizing the birdcage was actually a bird and returning her gaze to the path ahead.

Heartbroken

"For goodness sake!" the White Rabbit said. "Why would they come into such a place? This forest is filled with the strangest creatures, the signs on the trees are nonsensical, there is no practicality to this place whatsoever. We're going to get as lost as they are if we venture farther in. I must insist we go back to the castle and send your guards to find them, Your Majesty." The White Rabbit looked stern, and rather serious. It was not the first time she saw him look so resolute, but it surprised her nevertheless. It would be a look that would come over him more and more as the years went on.

"It is not your place to insist upon anything, Little Rabbit, but I do appreciate your concern. At least I know there is one person in this kingdom who cares for me." She smiled at her friend.

"I'm not exactly a person, Your Majesty, but I take your calling me so as a compliment."

"Come, Rabbit, let's make our way," she said, smiling again and hoping he wasn't offended. She had already come to think of this rabbit as her friend, and she hoped if she *had* offended him he would feel he

Tulgey Wood

could tell her. He did seem to be taking liberties in every other way.

The Queen of Hearts and White Rabbit followed the trail down a long path—past a number of unusual birds, which, as far as they could tell, did not speak and were therefore of no help whatsoever—that led into the darkest part of the forest. Here the trees were not colorful, they were black like charcoal and smelled of sulfur. The Queen and rabbit could no longer see the servants' tracks, not only because the sun had fully set but because the forest floor was scorched and blackened.

It was rather unpleasant to walk among the brittle, burnt trees, the black ash drifting down from their branches like something from a nightmare. The farther they ventured into the forest the thicker the air, and soon the White Rabbit was no longer white but gray.

"This couldn't be the right way, Your Majesty. And even if it were, it certainly couldn't be safe. I must insist we turn back for your safety."

"What did I say about insisting, Rabbit? I'm not

Heartbroken

sure it's your place." The Queen sighed. "But in this case, as usual, you are right. Perhaps we should return in the light of day. I'm afraid it's too dark to see anything at all."

But the Queen and the rabbit had lost their bearings and couldn't recall from which direction they had come, and they had no means to retrace their steps back. There was so little light in the blackened forest, and they had no choice other than to stand in place and contemplate what to do next.

"Do you smell that? Is it smoke?" The rabbit sniffed the air, his nose and whiskers twitching. The Queen found it funny, seeing the rabbit sniff like that. It was the most rabbity thing he had done since they met. She wasn't even sure at what point she stopped thinking of him as a rabbit, but the sight of him sniffing the air reminded her he wasn't, in fact, a person at all.

"Well, of course it's smoke, Rabbit. Clearly there has been a fire here."

"No, I mean, it smells as if one is still burning. Look! Over there." He pointed a paw toward a

Tulgey Wood

smoldering orange glow in the darkness. And before the Queen knew what was happening, the rabbit had dashed off down the wooded path, out of the Queen's sight.

Another rabbity thing to do.

"Rabbit, be careful!" she called after him. She feared her little friend was right. Perhaps venturing into these woods wasn't the best of choices, even if she was there with the best of intentions. One of the things she had learned on this adventure was that intentions sometimes did not matter. Which seemed like a strange thing to think. Of course, it was preferable for everyone to have the best of intentions, and in that sense, she supposed intentions mattered. But what of the times when you were well intended, and everything went awry?

This day was an example of good intentions going very badly. How could she have known that attempting to greet and deliver cakes to all her subjects would turn out to be such a disaster? Not all of it was her fault, of course. The Tweedle brothers and the Caterpillar were insufferable, to be sure, but then again, she and the rabbit wouldn't have had so much fun growing and shrinking if they hadn't set out to explore this land. And if it hadn't been for this day, she and the rabbit might not have become friends. So she decided it wasn't so bad after all. Not entirely bad, not really, all things considered. But then again, the Queen of Hearts worried that she hadn't yet seen the worst of this day and opted to wait until she was safe in her castle before deciding if good intentions mattered or not.

"My Queen! My Queen! Come quick. You must see this!" The Queen could hear panic in the rabbit's voice. She took tentative steps in his direction, dreading what she might find when she got there.

The forest was almost entirely dark now, except for the light emanating from the smoldering pile of wood that cast an eerie amber light on the White Rabbit. She could hardly see him, the air was so thick with smoke and ash, but she could tell by his wide and frightened eyes that something was horribly amiss.

"What is it, Rabbit? What have you found?" She was coughing and gasping for air, and her eyes were

Tulgey Wood

watering. She tried to wipe them with the cuff of her sleeve, but it only made her eyes sting more.

"I believe it's our cart, Your Majesty."

"I don't understand, Rabbit. What's happened?" She couldn't see properly. Her eyes were streaming with tears from the smoke and ash.

"Blast this horrible place!" she said, stamping her foot. "I hate it! I hate it here! It's the worst place ever!" Her face once again grew red, and she felt as though steam were coming out of her ears. She supposed the rage inside her had to go somewhere.

"Don't cry, Your Majesty. It's not your fault."

"Of course it's not my fault, Rabbit. I didn't start the fire. And I am not crying. Queens don't cry. The smoke is making my eyes water."

"Oh! Here," said the rabbit, handing her his pocket square. "Use this."

"You really are quite the gentlerabbit, aren't you?" she said, taking the pocket square and wiping her eyes. "Thank you, Rabbit. That's much better." Finally, she was able to see why the rabbit was in such a state. She couldn't quite take it in. He was right. It *was* their cart, and the servants were gone.

"Oh, this is awful, Rabbit. Where are the servants? This is all my fault. My very first day as Queen, and I've made a mess of everything!"

"This is not your fault, my Queen!"

"Of course it is! I am their Queen!" This time she was crying, and she was panicking. She felt panic and shame flooding her body, making her heart race, making her feel like she wanted to escape her own body. She hated feeling this way. Hated that it felt like anger. "They're dead! They're dead! How could I be so foolish, taking them along on an excursion into a world we know nothing about? They would be safe in the castle right now if I hadn't insisted we deliver cakes to a bunch of ungrateful lunatics! What was I thinking?"

"Your Majesty, stop! Look at me. You didn't command them to go into the woods!"

"Indeed I did not!" she said, looking into the rabbit's kind and wise eyes and feeling a bit calmer.

"Then how are you to blame for their blundering into this decrepit forest? For all we know, they

Tulgey Wood

escaped whatever happened and are now back at the castle awaiting our return." The rabbit took both of the Queen's hands in his furry white paws and squeezed them. "Everything will be okay. I'm sure they are fine."

"The fact is you don't really know that, but I appreciate . . . Wait. What is that?" The Queen noticed a flickering light in her periphery, a small lick of flames appearing in the tree branches to her right.

"What is that?" she asked again, spinning around. The forest exploded with light as all of the surrounding trees burst into dancing flames. But what was even more frightening was the thundering noise that shook the ground beneath them.

The Queen screamed, "Rabbit, look!" The entire forest before them was engulfed in flames. She could feel the heat even though the fire was a good distance away. They both stood there, unable to move, as the flames grew and diminished in intensity, as the forest floor shook, causing the flames in trees to quiver. And from the flames emerged a great beast, surely some sort of winged dragon, silhouetted in the distance, flames erupting from its mouth. The ground shook more violently as the creature moved nearer, causing the blackened trees above them to crumble and rain down ash. The Queen's mouth opened in surprise to see that, rather than go out, the flames continued to hover in the empty black sky where the disintegrated tree branches used to be.

"What is the meaning of this?" The dancing flames seemed to be suspended by magic; it didn't make sense. And again, the Queen felt as if she must be dreaming herself, or trapped within someone else's dream. Everything she had experienced that day was inconceivable, and she didn't understand why she was still living in this nightmare, for surely that was what it had to be.

"They're birds, Your Majesty."

"Birds? Impossible," she whispered, mesmerized by the beauty and horror of what she was seeing.

"They're birds, with mirrored faces! They're simply reflecting the fire. Now come on!" He took the Queen by the hand and darted away.

Tulgey Wood

They made their escape as quickly as they could, not daring to look back or stop to ogle the perplexing menagerie of creatures who resided in the woods. They just kept moving until they found a path that led somewhere, and a path to anywhere seemed better than standing still nowhere, so they followed it. But no matter how fast they ran they could still hear the dragon keeping pace behind them, roaring and blowing its fire that never quite reached them, until finally they were clear of the woods, out of breath and exhausted.

The Queen was doubled over in pain, holding her side and gasping for breath. She was unable to run any farther, even though the White Rabbit was tugging at her arm and urging her to keep moving.

"I can't go on, Rabbit. I don't think I'm someone who is used to running. It hurts. . . ."

"We can't stop, Your Majesty, the dragon is still coming!" The rabbit was panting and thumping his leg nervously, but she truly couldn't go on. She couldn't stop coughing, and it was so hard for her to breathe.

Heartbroken

"Oh, the Jabberwock? Don't worry about him, he rarely comes out of the woods. Not unless he has to." The voice came from nowhere and everywhere at once, and the Queen wasn't convinced it was friendly. For all they knew it was the dragon playing games with them, trying to trick or frighten them from within the darkness of the woods.

"Hello? Who's there? Show yourself!" The Queen spun in circles, trying to find where the voice was coming from, but she saw no one other than the White Rabbit, who was terrified, his small eyes wide with worry. "Rabbit, please calm down. I think we're okay." The Queen pulled the rabbit closer to her and put her arms around him. "Your heart is racing. Please, my Little Rabbit, please calm yourself."

"But where is that voice coming from?" The poor rabbit was stammering, and trembling in fear.

"I don't know my little friend, but I will protect you," she said, squinting down the forest path and seeing nothing but darkness. There were no flames, no dragon, and the ground was no longer shaking.

Tulgey Wood

"Over here, Your Majesty," said the voice. "In the woods." And then she saw it, a wide glowing grin in the darkness, floating like one of the birds with mirrors for faces.

"Get back, Rabbit! Run!" Instinctively, the Queen put her body between his and the eerie floating smile. "Stay back, dragon! I demand you go back into the forest where you belong!"

"I am no dragon, my Queen, I assure you," said the voice, and as it spoke, a face materialized, and then a body, and soon she was looking at a plump pink-and-purple striped cat with a wide Cheshire grin. It was sitting on the branch of a tree right at the edge of the dark forest.

"Well, that is plain, but *who are you?*" asked the Queen, looking down at the state of her dress, now covered in black soot, realizing how she must appear after her encounter with the dragon. She could only imagine what her face and hair looked like, and here she was meeting one of her subjects for the first time. What would he make of her? But she decided it didn't matter considering she could look far worse if

Heartbroken

she had been charred to death by the beastly dragon in the woods.

"You sound like the Caterpillar," the cat said as its grin grew wider. The Queen laughed despite herself. She supposed she did sound like that disgusting butterfly larva, yet she still took note that the cat did not answer her question. But no matter, there were more important questions that needed answering.

"Excuse me, Mr. Cat, but did you by chance see a group of servants passing through here? Perhaps running toward the castle?" She narrowed her eyes at him, trying to determine if he was the sort of creature who told the truth—being a creature with a perpetual smile on his face led her to think he might not be entirely trustworthy.

"I did not. Though I did hear a group of people making grim noises in the woods not too long before you came running," said the cat, wrapping his tail around his face to hide his grin.

"Oh dear." The Queen felt herself turning from red to white as the blood drained from her face.

"Don't fret, Your Majesty. Perhaps Mr. Cat is

Tulgey Wood

mistaken, and the servants got away," said the rabbit, who had finally seemed to find his courage, coming out from behind the Queen.

"If I were to guess," said the cat, "and I do so love guessing, I would say they didn't get away, and that is why the Jabberwock didn't follow you out of the forest." The Queen hated the way the cat smiled when he said that, as if he took delight in the idea of her servants being burned to a crisp or eaten alive. Then again, it seemed he really only had one expression. Of course, she couldn't be sure whether that was the case, but so far, she had only seen his long, wide grin, no matter how dire his words.

"I distinctly heard you say the Jabberwock isn't known for venturing out of the woods," said the rabbit. The Queen took note that he was already agitated with the cat, and she might have been too if she thought the cat was capable of saying anything without smiling.

"As I said, he isn't, not usually, anyway, unless he has to. And I'm guessing he didn't have to because he was already full, having just made a meal of your servants."

Heartbroken

"Oh, this is too awful! It's too much!"

"Too much for what?" asked the cat, swishing his tail and revealing his smile again. The Queen had the impression this cat was taunting her on purpose. But why would this creature, whom she had only just met mere moments ago, go out of his way to taunt her? More than likely she was just imagining things.

"It's just too much! All of it! It's too much to bear! This really is the worst place. I hate it, I say! I hate it!"

"Calm down, Your Majesty. We need to find you a place to rest and compose yourself." The rabbit looked around to see if there was a place nearby where they could rest.

"Yes, I believe composure is high on the list of virtues befitting a queen," said the cat.

"Well, I say compassion should be high on the list of virtues befitting a talking cat!" said the Queen.

"Have you met many talking cats?" asked the grinning feline.

"I can't say that I have," she said, realizing she couldn't remember meeting any sort of cat yet somehow still knew all about them, and knew they didn't usually talk. Of course, she had no idea how she knew this. She supposed it was akin to the White Rabbit knowing everything there was to know about how royal households worked but not remembering how. Yet as it was, they could both be wrong about the things they thought they knew because here she was, arguing with a talking cat.

"I can't say if I have ever met a talking cat, either. You say I lack compassion, but would you rather I said your servants had escaped when they did not? Give you false hope only for you to wonder what befell them? And how would you ever trust me again, weaving such lies?"

"I suppose you're right, Cat. Thank you for your honesty." The Queen thought there was some wisdom in that. Perhaps she was just letting her temper get the best of her. She had already done so on many occasions that day, even before her servants were likely eaten by a dragon.

"Did I hear correctly that you were delivering cakes today? The Tweedles came rambling through the woods rumbling and grumbling about queens, cakes, ravens, and rattles."

"I don't suppose it was the Tweedles you heard screaming, and not my servants?" asked the Queen, wondering how they managed to make their way past the cat when they went in the other direction at the crossroads, but there was very little she knew about this place, or the creatures who lived within it, and she decided it was best not to question such things, especially when there were more pressing issues at hand, like the fates of her servants.

"I'm afraid not, Your Majesty," said the cat, smiling even more widely and swishing his tail rather dramatically. "The Tweedles are fighting fit. So, now that we have that sorted, tell me about these *cakes*!"

"Do talking cats like cake?" she asked.

"Well, even though I can speak, I cannot speak for all talking cats, provided I am not unique in those qualities, but I can say without a doubt that this talking cat loves cake."

"Well, that's a lovely surprise. I was afraid you

would turn your nose up at it like the Caterpillar. To be honest, he was quite rude."

"The Caterpillar turns his nose up at almost everything. Though strictly speaking, I am not sure, being a caterpillar, he *has* a nose. Nevertheless, I wouldn't let it vex you, unless of course you enjoy being vexed."

"Why would it vex me to learn caterpillars do not have noses? And why would I enjoy being vexed?" she asked, trying to hide that she was, in fact, vexed.

"It's just a feeling," said the grinning cat. "A spark I see within. A small smoldering ember glowing, just waiting to burst."

"I'm curious if you have ever met this particular caterpillar, Mr. Cat, because I distinctly remember he had something that looked very much like a nose, and I assure you he did turn it up. As for other caterpillars, I couldn't say if they do or do not have noses, since I have to my knowledge only met one."

The Queen felt her annoyance turning to anger, and she wanted to admonish him for daring speak to his Queen in such a familiar way. But she was determined to be polite. She was determined to make at least one friend this day aside from the White Rabbit.

"Well, now that I know at least one talking cat enjoys cake, I would love nothing more than for you to join me for tea and cake at my castle," she continued, trying her best to be congenial. The last thing she wanted was to prove this cat right.

"And my mistress," he said slyly, "is she welcome?"

"And who might that be?" the Queen asked, wondering how it was possible for such a cat to have a mistress when he seemed exactly like the sort of cat who did what he pleased.

"The Duchess, of course."

"Of course, she would be most welcome," said the Queen, having no idea who this Duchess was but nevertheless trying her best to be polite. She quickly reasoned the polite and queenly thing to do was to invite the Duchess and her cat over for tea.

"Your Majesty, it is quite late, and it's well after dark. We really should get you back to the castle."

"Indeed, Rabbit! It was nice meeting you, Cat.

I look forward to meeting your mistress." With that, the Queen took the rabbit's hand and turned to leave.

"And the baby," said the cat, making her turn around and look at him.

"I'm sorry, what? Did you say baby?"

"Yes, the baby, she is never without it."

"Then I insist she bring the baby."

"Wonderful. We will keep an eye out for your invitation."

"Please do!" said the Queen as she and the White Rabbit made their way back, finding the path that would lead them to the castle. But soon her agitation with the cat turned to nervousness. And she could hardly think clearly with the sound of singing coming from a nearby garden as they walked past. Every now and then the singing would pause, and two voices would shout back and forth:

"A very merry unbirthday, to you . . ."

"And a very merry unbirthday to YOU!"

"What in Wonderland is an unbirthday?" The Queen asked.

Heartbroken

"I couldn't tell you, Your Majesty. Best to just ignore it and go straight to the castle."

"I suppose whoever they are, they wouldn't have turned down our cake—they seem very celebratory. Then again, who knows if there is cake at an unbirthday party? Imagine, if cake were involved in an unbirthday celebration, would that mean having cake almost every day? Now I wish we still had our cakes."

"And the servants."

"Yes, of course. The servants, too. But do you think the people singing in the garden would like a cake?"

"It's hard to say. I shall investigate these ponderations and report back to you in the coming days."

"I wouldn't object to a similar report on everyone in my queendom."

"I suspected as much, Your Majesty."

"You're too good to me, Rabbit. To be honest, I am dreading going back to the castle. How will I tell the other servants what happened?"

"Why don't you leave that to me, Your Majesty?"

Tulgey Wood

"Would you really do that, Rabbit?"

"It is my duty to serve you, my Queen."

"Only if you want to, Rabbit. Only if it would make you happy."

"Nothing would make me happier. Besides, I don't think I have anywhere else to go."

"That's right! Today is your first day, too! Well, in that case, please call the castle your home. We will find you the grandest of quarters, and a fine office, and since you are of unusual size for a rabbit now you shouldn't have trouble managing the furniture."

"Don't forget, my Queen, I am a rabbit and I can jump!" he said, laughing.

But the Queen did not share in his laughter. She kept thinking about her servants, and how terrible it must have been to be gobbled up by a dragon. She couldn't think how she could possibly tell the King about this; she kept scripting it over and over in her mind, but nothing felt like it captured the true horror of the situation. Nothing conveyed her guilt adequately, and she wondered how she would face him, or the other servants. She felt herself falling into a dark place of fear and anxiety, apprehensive about what would happen next.

"My Queen, we may not have achieved everything we set out to do this day, but I think we did come up with a name for this place. Wonderland! What do you think of it?"

"I think it's perfect!" The rabbit's brilliance continued to dazzle her. What better name could there be besides Wonderland? She had done nothing but wonder at its perplexities, annoyances, vexations, and tomfoolery since she arrived. "Wonderland indeed!"

"Brilliant, then we did one good thing today."

"More than one, I should think," she said, feeling once again emboldened by the rabbit's encouraging words. "We have now, in our possession, incredible growing and shrinking potions; we made friends with a talking cat, and quite possibly a duchess, and, improbably, a baby; and now we know never again to set foot in Tulgey Wood."

"We should put up a sign warning travelers not to enter," he said.

"Capital idea, Rabbit. Now let's go home."

Chapter VII

The Duchess

The Queen's next few days in Wonderland went slightly better than her first, but only because she didn't leave the castle. Instead, she familiarized herself with the grounds, her staff, and her guard, and she tried to get to know the King but quickly grew bored of that fruitless endeavor. Instead, she occupied herself by planning a lavish tea for the Duchess, her cat, and apparently her baby. The Queen had no idea how one would host a baby and hoped the Duchess would be content to have one of the maids look after it while they enjoyed their tea. As for the cat, she was looking forward to chatting with him further. She hadn't yet decided if she disliked his cheeky behavior, and she savored the idea of getting to know him and his intentions better.

Since it had been only a handful of days at most since her first, not much else transpired aside from the planning of the tea and listening to the White Rabbit's reports about the various inhabitants of Wonderland he had managed to compile in those few short days. It would take some time before he could meet everyone in her queendom and give the Queen their stories; perhaps the Duchess would provide some of her own impressions.

She arranged for tea to be served in the solarium. She was expecting the Duchess and her entourage at any moment. The servants had set out a number of delicious-looking cakes and a rather plump teapot with a black-and-white checkered pattern. The cups were red, the saucers were black, and the little cake plates matched the teapot. The Queen would never have thought of mixing and matching the saucers, teacups, and plates, but it worked beautifully. There were all sizes of cakes set out, in more flavors than one could possibly try in a day. There were tiny little lemon cakes, lavender cakes, large chocolate cakes, coconut cakes, cakes with pink marzipan, cakes with little purple flowers, hazelnut cakes, spiced cakes, and brandy-soaked fruitcakes. So many cakes. They had also made a delicious assortment of tea sandwiches and scones, with little pots of clotted cream and lemon curd, as well as little round cookies that had heart-shaped jam centers.

The Queen could hardly choose from the number of astounding dresses she found in her bedchamber wardrobe. She hadn't remembered this about herself, but apparently she had very good taste! At last she settled on a dress she felt suited the occasion, along with the jewels to match. The Queen wore a particularly beautiful dress, wanting to make an impression on the Duchess. It was a black velvet dress with delicately embroidered red hearts, and a gold circlet with ruby hearts. When she got downstairs she went about the room checking everything was just right for the arrival of the Duchess, making sure to place the beautiful confections just so, and trying to ignore the chilly attitude of her servants.

Ever since she and the rabbit arrived back to the castle on the evening of their ill-fated adventure in Tulgey Wood, none of the servants looked the Queen in the eye. It had been less than a week since their misadventure, and it was clear the servants were still feeling the sting of the loss of their friends. But the Queen didn't understand why they were avoiding her gaze. The White Rabbit assured her that was the usual protocol, and not one single person held her responsible for the nasty encounter with the dragon. Yet she couldn't help but feel the servants did indeed blame her, and though she had only admitted it to the White Rabbit, she shared their opinion.

The White Rabbit had not only spared her from having to break the news to the servants, but he had also spared her from having to face the King that evening. The King seemed agreeable when the White Rabbit informed him that the Queen was far too exhausted after her ordeal and that she would be

The Duchess

going straight to her own bedchamber, explaining that the maids would prepare a separate bedchamber for him. The Queen loved how the rabbit could make anything sound official, as if he was the authority on courtly rules and proper protocols. When the Queen thought about it, sleeping in separate rooms did sound like something kings and queens did, and since the King did not object, the Queen had to assume the White Rabbit knew what he was talking about, or at the very least was very good at sounding like he knew what he was talking about.

The Queen was having trouble adjusting to life in the castle, especially with the servants giving her the side-eye and whispering about her when they thought she wasn't looking. It took some persuading, but she had finally gotten it out of the rabbit that the entire kitchen went into a panic when she ordered so many cakes for the Duchess's visit. She realized it was thoughtless of her, ordering so many, and it was no wonder they were convinced she was going to march them off to Tulgey Wood, where they would also be devoured by the dragon. It seemed no matter what she did it was always the wrong thing, which made her feel perpetually on edge. She found herself getting angry when the faces of her servants turned pale with fright when she spoke to them. She wanted to scream at them, *I AM NOT TRYING TO MURDER YOU, YOU FOOLS!* She kept her composure, but within it was like a storm brewing, desperate to come out. It almost *did* make her want to murder them, because holding in her anger all the time only seemed to make it more intense.

She supposed there were kings and queens who did such things like scream at their servants and threaten their lives, but she wasn't one of them. She couldn't imagine being that sort of ruler, maintaining order through fear and violence. The only person in her household the Queen wanted to be afraid of her was the King. And it wasn't as if he had done anything wrong, not really, she just didn't know him. And all things considered, that wasn't his fault, her not knowing him, but it didn't endear him to her, either.

She recalled a conversation she and the rabbit had

on one of their daily walks through the hedge maze, the only place in her queendom where she seemed to find a tiny measure of peace, away from the servants and most especially her husband.

"You know, Your Majesty, it's quite common for monarchs not to know each other before they are married. It's not unusual in the slightest."

"But we are married, Rabbit! And he knows me! He remembers me! He's in love with me, Rabbit, and I have no memory of him at all!"

"It could be worse, I suppose. He could know you and not love you. He could hate you, in fact."

"It's intolerable, Rabbit. He follows me around declaring his love, sending me trinkets and little poems. I hate to admit it, but it makes my skin crawl."

"He's in love with you. He can't help it."

"And I can't help that I find his attentions repulsive. He's too familiar. He's a stranger to me who takes too many liberties."

"I wonder how he remembers you, yet you don't remember him?"

"Who knows how anything in this infernal place

works, Rabbit? You seem to know how kingdoms, or rather queendoms, work, and those Tweedles seem to know . . . things . . . I suppose. And that hatmaker or whatever you said his name was seems to know all about unbirthday parties, and the cat, well, he seems to know far more than he's letting on."

"His name is the Mad Hatter. And you're right, some of the inhabitants do seem to know more than others. I hear the King is hunting in Tulgey Wood today. He's determined to slay the Jabberwock. That should keep him busy. Of course he will likely spend his evening alone, waiting for you to come to him."

"I know! I don't know what's wrong with me. He is truly kind and understanding, but I can't get past the terror of that first day, waking up beside a man I didn't know. I was convinced he was going to condemn me for what happened to the servants, but he showed me nothing but compassion."

"He didn't even say anything about how much taller you are than him."

"I know! There is a part of me that wants to remember him, to love him back, but I just can't,

The Duchess

Rabbit. I think we're too different. And if I am forced to be completely honest, he's boring, and rather annoying. Nothing seems to bother him. He's always so . . . happy. Always making the best of everything. He didn't even seem hurt when you told him I wanted separate rooms."

"I think he's waiting for you to remember him. Waiting for you to love him back."

"But what if I never remember?"

"Maybe he was too boring to remember," said the rabbit, making the Queen laugh.

"See! Now that's funny! You never bore me, rabbit."

The Queen's musings were interrupted by the White Rabbit coming into the room. She was suddenly transported from that day with the White Rabbit, walking in her garden maze, back to awaiting the Duchess in her solarium. The sight of the White Rabbit in the entryway took her off guard. He looked comical in the uniform he now wore when attending to official court duties. As he stood there in his white-and-red doublet with a great red heart

Heartbroken

in the center and his light blue ruffled collar, she wondered if he shouldn't just go back to wearing his usual tweed suit.

"Rabbit! Are you quite comfortable in that costume? I'm not sure it suits you."

"It is the proper attire for my duties, Your Majesty."

"Shouldn't I be the one who decides upon proper attire, Rabbit?"

"Indeed, Your Majesty. I only came in to let you know the King has gone out hunting today and hopes you will join him for dinner."

"Thank you, Rabbit. Perhaps I should. Do you think I have been unfair with him?"

"No, not unfair, Your Majesty, but you might find that if you get to know the King, your heart may soften to him. He does seem to love you a great deal."

"I think that is the problem, Rabbit. I don't know him. I don't even know myself. He loves me, and I have no idea why."

"Aren't you curious about your life together before your first day?"

The Duchess

"Fine, Rabbit, tell him I will have dinner with him this evening. Perhaps you can give him some hints on how not to be boring!" she said expecting the White Rabbit to laugh at her joke but instead his ears were twitching like he heard or sensed something she could not.

"I wonder, is that the Duchess's carriage I hear pulling up while we've been talking?" The White Rabbit was doing rabbity things again that reminded her that he was indeed a rabbit, and not a person, which amused her.

"I hope so, Rabbit. It may be by the end of the day I will have another new friend," the Queen said.

"Perhaps so. Now if you will excuse me, I must go greet the Duchess in the courtyard and escort her here."

But before the White Rabbit could make his way out of the room, the door burst open, revealing the most peculiar-looking woman the Queen would ever behold. Her eyes were too small and close together, and her ears were too large and stuck out like those of a bat. But the most remarkable aspect of her ill-favored looks was the size of her head and face, larger, in fact, than any the Queen had seen since she came to Wonderland. Emphasizing this, the Duchess wore an enormous headpiece with a long length of fabric that draped over her shoulders. And to make matters worse, she was holding a screaming baby, and standing beside her was, by all estimations, her cook, though why the Duchess would bring her own cook was beyond the Queen.

In the short time the Queen had known the White Rabbit, she had learned he didn't like this sort of thing, going against protocol—barging in unannounced, bringing a cook into the solarium—but she hoped he wouldn't offend the Duchess upon their very first acquaintance with one of his scolding remarks. Before the White Rabbit could say anything, however, the Duchess took over the room.

"By the looks on your faces, I think introductions are in order," she announced, speaking loudly to be heard over the sounds of her screaming baby. The Queen had never heard a baby cry that shrilly before. In fact, she wasn't sure she had ever met a baby, or

The Duchess

heard one cry, and she decided it wasn't at all agreeable. "I am the Duchess, this is my baby, and this is my cook. She is here to make sure everything is to my liking." The Queen thought this to be rather rude, since the Duchess was a guest in her castle, and she was, after all, the Queen, but she was determined not to let this day fall into chaos. She was determined not to lose her temper. She would let this lack of decorum go unremarked upon, even though she found it rather remarkable.

"I assure you, Duchess," the White Rabbit said, all decorum, "there is no need for this. The Queen has the finest cooks and bakers in the land." Despite his calm demeanor, the White Rabbit's foot was thumping in what the Queen perceived to be slight agitation, and his nose was wrinkled in what she could only imagine was distaste. She hoped the rabbit would hold his temper; if one of them was to explode in rage, she rather thought it should be her, the Queen.

"Well, that may have been true, but rumor has it that the Queen went and got many of her staff eaten

Heartbroken

by the Jabberwock, and so one can't be too careful." The Duchess laughed at her own remark, as if she thought it was the funniest joke she had ever heard rather than one in very poor taste, if it could be called a joke at all. But the Duchess didn't stop there, she just kept talking while promenading around the room, not letting the Queen or the White Rabbit get a word in edgewise.

"It's like I said to my cat: there's no telling who she has down in her kitchens cooking and baking now, so it's best not to chance it." This was absurd, as it was hardly seemly to bring one's cooks and bakers on a journey to deliver their own cakes, and it was indeed her travel entourage who had—possibly—been eaten. The Queen's blood began to boil. As the Duchess circled the room remarking on this or that, she seemed to be looking for something. She flipped over pillows, looked under chairs, and peeked behind curtains, yet she seemed to come up empty-handed. When it was clear she had not found what she was seeking, she stopped and looked at the Queen with disgust.

The Duchess

"No king?" Her face twisted with a nasty smirk.

"Is that what you were looking for?" the Queen asked in surprise. "The King? Do you expect to find him under a pillow?"

"Well, I did hear he is smaller than you. Is he not? After your escapades with the potions. Well, if he's not here, I daresay he must be out hunting the dragon again. I suppose *someone* has to do something about the menace," said the Duchess. The Queen and the rabbit just stared at her in awe, watching her act as though it was the most normal thing in the world to be behaving so rudely while her baby wailed—also rudely, if the Queen was to be honest about it. It was true she didn't remember much, but it did seem common sense not to cry the whole time when someone has invited you for lunch.

"Excuse me, Duchess, but it was the Queen who commanded the King to hunt the beast," said the rabbit, his foot thumping even faster.

"Indeed? Well, I suspect the Red Queen will be very interested to hear that," said the Duchess, giving the Queen a strange look. The Queen found all of this very odd. Not that she should have expected differently, after everything she had already experienced in this confounding, infuriating place. But she had assumed someone with the title of Duchess would understand proper decorum, and the fact that the opposite was true did take her by surprise.

The Queen wanted to ask who this *other* queen, this Red Queen, was, and why she would care if the King of Hearts hunted the Jabberwock. She wanted to ask what gave the Duchess the right to come into her castle and insult her, but she was speechless. It was all she could do to pay attention to the insipid words coming from the Duchess's mouth. The Queen of Hearts found the Duchess to be an exceedingly distracting and vexing woman, not only crass and ill-mannered, but also ill-proportioned in every way. But the Duchess's unsightly looks and rude demeanor were not the only reasons the Queen was distracted from what this odious and grotesque woman was saying; it was the squealing baby squirming in the Duchess's arms. The Queen, as far she knew, had never been in the company of a baby, and upon first impressions she decided that was probably for the best. In fact, she was becoming more sure with every passing moment that she detested babies, and she could see the rabbit had noticed her revulsion by the expression on her face.

"Why don't I show your cook to the kitchens and have one of the maids take care of the baby so you may enjoy your tea," said the rabbit, pulling the cord for the maid while at the same time giving the Queen a look that communicated he wasn't sure it was wise to continue in this folly, but he would follow through on his royal duties until told otherwise.

"And where is your talking cat?" asked the Queen, trying to move the conversation in another direction. The last thing she wanted was to get into a row with the Duchess. She was nobility, after all, as far as she knew, anyway, though she would later wonder if the Duchess hadn't just named herself thus in the same mad way everyone in Wonderland gave themselves various titles at whim.

"My cat? Oh, he's probably around here somewhere. He will appear when it suits him. He always does." She thrust the baby into the maid's arms the moment she walked into the room.

"And Cook, before you go, please inspect the food and make sure it is up to our usual standards. Then you may go downstairs with the other servants," said the Duchess.

"Of course, Your Grace," said the cook as she took a comically large pepper shaker out of her bag. Before the rabbit could do anything to stop her, the cook proceeded to generously pepper all of the cakes and sandwiches, and even went so far as to take the lid off the teapot and pepper the tea as well. The Queen was convinced this was some sort of prank. That, or the Duchess and her cook were suffering from an uneasiness of the mind, because the Duchess just stood there watching her cook shake more and more pepper as if it was the most normal thing in the world, until at last the rabbit was forced to take matters into his own paws.

"What exactly are you doing, madam?" The Queen loved the rabbit's look of outrage. And she loved that he was always there in her defense.

The Duchess

"Peppering the cakes, of course! You can't expect the Duchess to eat cakes without pepper!" The rabbit's question seemed to cause the cook to shake the pepper more vigorously than before, as if she knew her peppering was coming to an end and she needed to make sure she peppered everything enough before she was sent out of the room.

"I must insist you cease this peppering at once! How dare you take such liberties!" said the rabbit, snatching the pepper shaker out of the cook's hand.

"Hand over that pepper at once!" The Duchess bounded across the room and grabbed the rabbit by the scruff of his furry white neck. In that moment, it felt like the floodgates opened within the Queen. Without even thinking, she grabbed the Duchess by her long veil and yanked it so hard, it pulled her headdress and wig right off her head. The Duchess cried out and released the White Rabbit, who staggered backward, almost losing his footing.

"Unhand my rabbit, Duchess, or I will have your head!" said the Queen, suddenly unable to control the outburst. As soon as it was out of her mouth, she couldn't believe she had said it. Even the rabbit looked twitchy.

"Did you just threaten me?" asked the Duchess, smashing the pepper shaker to the ground in a shatter of glass. Everything was in chaos. The room was filled with pepper, the Duchess was angrily scrambling to replace her wig and headdress, and the baby was still wailing in the arms of the maid, who stood there in shock at the spectacle.

"Indeed I did, you odious woman. Look at you crawling on the floor, like the wretched creature you are! How dare you come into my castle and pepper me with insults, and my cakes with, well, pepper! And worst of all, you mistreat my rabbit? Well, I won't have it! I order you, your deranged cook, and your infuriating baby to leave my castle at once! And if you *ever* threaten my rabbit again, I will have your head on a pike!"

"I'm not sure we have pikes sturdy enough to hold the Duchess's head, Your Majesty," said the rabbit, eyeing the enormous headdress, which the Duchess still struggled to replace.

The Duchess

"Indeed! Tell the smithy we are in need of sturdier pikes, then, Rabbit. And call for the guards to escort these miscreants to their carriage." The Queen covered her mouth to stifle the laugh that threatened to bubble up as she imagined the Duchess's head on a pike with her wig and headpiece askew.

"I have never been so humiliated, or treated so poorly, by anyone living! And look what you've done to my baby—you've made my precious snookums sneeze!" The Duchess was in a state of frenzy, cooing over her baby, who had not, in fact, sneezed.

"Your baby isn't sneezing," the Queen scoffed. "Though for the first time since you walked into this room, it's stopped crying." But before she could say more, the baby *did* sneeze, and in such rapid and violent succession the Queen was afraid the baby would sneeze itself out of the maid's arms.

"See! I told you, you've made my baby sneeze!"

"I did no such thing! It's all this pepper! And who puts pepper on cakes, anyway? Oh, this place is outrageous. Men in funny little hats fighting over a rattle, a high-handed caterpillar, murderous dragons, talking cats, and now a cake-peppering, rabbit-abusing duchess with a shape-shifting baby who turns into a pig!"

"*Pig?* You dare call my sweet snookums a pig? How dare you!"

The accounts of what happened next would differ depending on who was telling the story. If one were to believe the Duchess, the maid dropped the baby on the floor when, according to the maid, it sprang as a pig from her arms with a great sneeze and scrambled all over the room. Everything was in chaos, and as the Duchess chased after the pig, or the baby, depending on which story you heard, she managed to knock over the tables and chairs and to break most of the teacups. By anyone's account, as everyone in the room would agree, the tea party was a disaster, and despite the Queen's previous hopes, no friendship was formed that day. In fact, never again would the Duchess, her baby, or her cook ever step foot in the Queen's castle.

As the Queen of Hearts and the White Rabbit stood there amid the mess the Duchess left behind, they both sighed.

The Duchess

"Remind me, Rabbit, to never again trust talking cats with Cheshire grins." She shook her head looking at all the overturned teacups, spilled tea, and ruined cakes.

"Do you think this is what the Cheshire Cat intended, Your Majesty?"

"I do now. This is further evidence not to trust anyone charming in Wonderland. You are the only one here I can trust, Rabbit."

"How about the King? I have a feeling you can trust him. Will you give him a chance?"

"I don't know, Rabbit. I don't think I'm ready. As for this evening, please tell him I've had a trying day and would prefer to dine alone."

"As you wish, Your Majesty." The Queen could see the White Rabbit was disappointed, but she didn't want to face the King, not just yet.

"This isn't your fault, Little Rabbit. Neither of us could have expected the mayhem that befell us this day." She paused, thinking further. "Or perhaps we could have expected it, but didn't want to believe it."

"True, but I do feel in the future we should take

an extra modicum of precaution when inviting guests to tea, or when venturing out."

"I think you're right, Rabbit. But then again, what would be the fun in that?" she said, making the rabbit laugh with her cheeky grin. Something about the White Rabbit made her able to reach into herself and find even the tiniest glimmers of frivolity.

"Your Majesty, the King did ask me to give you a small gift. I'm not sure this is the right moment, but he was very excited for you to have them." With a flourish, he handed her a small black box with a red ribbon and a heart-shaped tag.

She took the box from his paw and opened it, revealing a pair of gold earrings that resembled long teardrops. They were rather unremarkable, rather plain, really, and she couldn't understand why he was so excited to give them to her. They were not exactly befitting a queen, at least she did not think so.

"He said he got them from some mysterious figure or another and was planning to tell you the story at dinner. It's a wild tale. He says witches are involved."

The Duchess

"That's all I need, cursed earrings."

"I didn't say anything about the earrings being cursed. You have a suspicious turn of mind. Won't you let the King tell you the story behind the earrings himself, tonight at dinner?"

"Good try, Rabbit. You can tell the King he is welcome to wear the cursed earrings if he wishes, but I don't intend to take any chances."

"Your Majesty!"

"Don't *Your Majesty* me! Put them with the other rubbish he's given me and ask someone to clean up this mess. And tell the cooks I don't want to see a speck of pepper on this evening's meal."

"Is there anything else I can do for you, my Queen?"

"Yes, Rabbit, I could use a hug."

Chapter VIII

A Letter from the White Queen

The White Queen's letter came early one morning while the Queen of Hearts was still in her bedchamber. The White Rabbit came upon her while she was having her morning tea and nibbling on the corners of her toast, a strange new custom the White Rabbit had taken note of. The Queen seemed in a jolly mood, likely because she hadn't yet had to speak with anyone that day, not even the maid who brought in her tea and toast.

It had been quite some time since the Duchess, cook, and pig visited the castle. How much time, exactly, was a meaningless question, especially in a

A Letter from the White Queen

place like Wonderland. What wasn't so meaningless was that the Queen didn't speak to the servants now unless she had to, and really, she never encountered such an occasion, thanks to the White Rabbit, who was always willing to speak with them on her behalf.

Ever since the Queen's first day, when everything went terribly wrong in Tulgey Wood, she had become convinced the servants didn't trust her, and no amount of pleasantries, afternoons off, or genteel deportment swayed their opinion of her. And since the White Rabbit was a gentlerabbit, he tried to shield the Queen from these truths because he knew they would upset her.

But there was no way to shield her from the letter that had arrived at the castle that morning from the White Queen. So, with a trembling paw, he took the letter from his pocket and handed it to the Queen of Hearts.

"What's this, Rabbit? This letter has already been opened. The seal is broken," she said, examining it front and back. "Ah, I see it was addressed to you. What does the White Queen want with my rabbit?"

Heartbroken

She had only gotten through the first line of the letter before she lost her temper.

"Well, this is pure nonsense! What is the meaning of this, issuing an arrest warrant for my rabbit! I assume her allegations are false." She looked at him, confused and angry, for confirmation.

"I couldn't say, Your Majesty, as you see, she's accused me of doing something in the future."

"This is folderol, pure nonsense, poppycock at the highest level!"

The Queen had gotten into the habit of using multiple words of similar meanings in the same statement. Since the Duchess's visit, she had become rattled and easily agitated with just about everyone except the White Rabbit, and in truth, he couldn't blame her.

Wonderland had proven to be a vexing and intolerable place. Nevertheless, she had done her best not to let the disasters that had befallen her thus far discourage her from inviting the other monarchs and subjects to a lavish ball that was open to all of her subjects. Even the Tweedle brothers, the Caterpillar, and the Cheshire Cat were among those invited; however, she couldn't bring herself to invite the Duchess, her cook, or the pig baby.

When she thought about her choices on her first day, she felt she had made some terrible mistakes. She should have never attempted to greet everyone in her kingdom on the very day she found herself in Wonderland. The White Rabbit *had* warned her. He said she should send out word to have everyone come to her, but she had been too excited. Too curious. And too impatient. What she hadn't taken into consideration was how angry she was. How scared, and anxious. Surely that was why everything went so wrong. And surely that was how she managed to make a disaster of her reign.

Since those early mishaps, she contented herself within her own castle and its grounds. She lived in sublime silence, unbothered by anyone, speaking to no one except for the White Rabbit. There was peace in that, tranquility and regulation. She was able to control her emotions without the vexations or bothers of the kingdom. The King saw to the daily duties of the court and the kingdom, and he knew not to share any of Wonderland's nonsense with her. She didn't want to hear about the fate of the oysters, or how the hatter was confused on the March Hare's actual birthday, or how the Mock Turtle was crying because he thought he was a real turtle.

The only news she ever received was from the White Rabbit, and only when she asked him. He was the one who told her the Duchess had been spreading gossip about her, the reason none of the monarchs had accepted her previous invitations to tea. But she soon began to feel remiss in her duties as queen and foolish for not setting things straight with the other kings and queens, leaving everything to her husband to deal with while she locked herself away from everyone for fear she would have another outburst like the one she'd unleashed on the Duchess. The truth was, she was afraid of her own anger, and she was doing everything she could to try to avoid succumbing to it. But at the same time, she knew she couldn't hide from her subjects forever. She needed to find a way to make peace with them and herself. Or at the

A Letter from the White Queen

very least find a way to tolerate them better. And of course, the White Rabbit encouraged this.

So together they planned the most spectacular ball, so enticing, and so magical, no one, not even her addle-brained subjects, would be able to say no. The Queen had Wonderland's jack-of-all-trades, Bill the Lizard, working around the clock to build the various outdoor stalls that would feature games in the gardens, as well as themed rooms throughout the castle. So elaborate were these creations, it was as if the entirety of Wonderland was replicated within the Queen's castle. Thanks to the White Rabbit's explorations around the queendom, he was able to learn everything there was to know about everyone in Wonderland. With only a few exceptions, there wasn't a person, talking animal, king, or queen he hadn't met and spoken to at length. And of course, he brought all this information back to the Queen, which did nothing to endear her to Wonderland or those who lived there and only succeeded in making her dislike the lot more.

Nevertheless the Queen made sure there would be

an enticement for everyone, and she spared no effort or expense. The morning room was decked out in an abundance of unbirthday decorations and gifts. There were no less than fifty teapots, all of them containing the hatter's and March Hare's favorite blends. And the Queen even reserved a number of empty teapots for the Dormouse, even though she had Bill construct a little house for the Dormouse in the shape of a teapot. The mouse-size dwelling opened like a dollhouse, and inside was a little kitchen, bedroom, and living room, each of them lavishly decorated for an unbirthday celebration.

In the music room, the Queen arranged a multitude of rattles for the Tweedles, all of them hanging from a replica of the tree where she had met them at the crossroads. She decided it was best not to invite the raven, but instead had Bill construct one from papier-mâché. Bill's papier-mâché skills were so good that she also had him construct the giant mushrooms, trees, and flowers for the Caterpillar's lair that showcased his new bejeweled hookah sitting proudly on the tallest of the mushrooms. And every

A Letter from the White Queen

room of the house had a different flowering tree for the Cheshire Cat to perch upon. They had scattered a number of chess tables around the castle for those who wished to play, and had a life-size chessboard constructed in the garden for those who wished to put themselves into play. And the White Rabbit, who observed the Queen of Hearts's recent obsession with card games, had a number of card tables and decks of cards for those who wished to indulge in a game with each other, and perhaps their Queen, who wouldn't be able to resist, especially if they wanted to play hearts.

Brilliantly, the Queen had sent the White Rabbit on a mission to inquire about everyone's favorite dishes, among the many other fact-finding expeditions she sent him on, and made sure they would have every single one in abundance. The tables in the dining hall were sagging under the weight of the various delights, and she was sure everyone would be enchanted by her thoughtfulness and meticulous planning.

The rabbit thought it was exceedingly brilliant of the Queen to cater to all of their guests' special interests, not only to tempt them to come to the party but to keep them happy and entertained while they were there. That was a quality of the Queen's the White Rabbit admired. She could be, when she wanted, a very thoughtful person, with the most vivid imagination and masterful intuition, and she was rather good at reading the natures of others, even if she didn't always apply these talents for her own betterment and well-being. Her talents really showed themselves in her planning of the Wonderland Ball, with a real eagerness to please everyone who attended down to the smallest detail. As far as the White Rabbit was concerned, there was no way the evening wouldn't be a success.

On the morning of the ball they walked around the castle together, inspecting all the rooms, sniffing all the cakes, making sure everything was just so, shaking the rattles, making sure the hookah was polished and gleaming. The Queen had even instructed Bill the Lizard to construct a special table for the dining hall, one that was not only enormous but also round so that none of the other monarchs would feel they were in a junior seat to the others—all equal to each other except, of course, to the Queen of Hearts, who would be seated on a red velvet back cushion in the shape of a voluptuous heart on an elaborate throne of dark wood. It would also not be missed that the entire castle was thoughtfully decorated with a great deal of heart embellishments. The gardens were hung with red paper-heart lanterns and red paper chains with dangling hearts, and every hall within the castle was bursting with red roses, the Queen's favorite flower.

The White Rabbit, also a keen observer of the nature of others, most specifically the Queen's, noticed that even though the Queen had gone out of her way to decorate the various rooms in the castle to her guests' special tastes, she hadn't thought about including something for herself, and it was he who made sure to include the card tables, roses, and hearts. He felt the act of mingling her roses and hearts alongside the other decorations that were so thoughtfully planned for her guests would maybe somehow bring them all together.

Heartbroken

"Well, if nothing else, at least they will know who is queen," she said, laughing.

But the smiles and laughter in the planning of the ball soon faded on the evening of the intended festivities. The White Rabbit would never forget the look on the Queen of Hearts's face that night, standing on the steps of her castle, eagerly awaiting her guests to pull up in their carriages. The entire guard was in attendance, lined up in smart uniforms denoting various suits in a deck of cards. The Queen had become rather preoccupied with card games, and cards themselves, so the White Rabbit thought it would be a good touch to have the guards wear uniforms to make themselves appear to be playing cards.

Everything was perfect, and the Queen's face was brimming with hope and anticipation for the evening. He could tell the Queen felt beautiful, and he had to agree. She wore a magnificent dress, red velvet covered in sparkling heart-shaped rubies, and a wig so large and impressive it was a work of art, expertly bedecked with lavish red roses, plumes, and more rubies to match her necklace and bracelets. As

A Letter from the White Queen

he looked across the courtyard, illuminated by red heart lanterns, the White Rabbit was filled with pride and excitement. He and his Queen had outdone themselves.

"You look so lovely this evening, Your Majesty."

"Thank you, Rabbit! You did a splendid job! I think this is going to be a grand party, I just know it!" She looked happier than he had seen her since their first day, when they had decided to explore Wonderland together.

"I was only following your brilliant orders."

"We did this together, my friend. By the way, what time do you have on your pocket watch?"

"A quarter or so past eight. But I daresay your guests are just fashionably late."

"Well, I'm not sure how fashionable they'll be, especially those Tweedle brothers."

She laughed behind her fan, but the White Rabbit could tell she was using humor and spite to cover her nervousness. He couldn't blame her for being nervous. She had not had one single encounter with a denizen of Wonderland that didn't end in vexation. Unless he counted himself, but the rabbit was sure that he wasn't from this foolhardy place any more than the Queen was. He thought she was rather brave, throwing this party, especially when the Wonderland residents had done nothing but agitate her, and he wondered if he had done the right thing in encouraging her. The last thing he wanted was to see her disappointed again, or risk her becoming angry and threatening to behead the whole kingdom like she had done with the Duchess. But when he heard her plans, saw all the trouble she went through, the attention to detail and how much she cared, he thought there was no way anyone who attended wouldn't have a splendid time. Maybe, just maybe, this would be a turning point for her. After tonight, she might even start to embrace her new home and role as queen.

"Perhaps clocks work differently here," she mused, checking the rabbit's pocket watch. "Maybe it wasn't clear on the invitation what time to arrive."

"That did cross my mind, Your Majesty. So I visited each of them myself and made sure to tell

A Letter from the White Queen

them what time to arrive and what you had planned, everything down to the last detail."

They stood there together a full hour, or more, before the Queen and rabbit reluctantly sent the guard back into the castle, coming to the conclusion no one was attending. Not a single person, talking animal, king, queen, or otherwise. It was heartbreaking for the rabbit to see all hope and excitement drain from the Queen's face and be replaced with heartbreak and disappointment.

"Why didn't they come, Rabbit?"

"I'm sure it's just some sort of Wonderland nonsense," he said, taking her into his arms. "The clock thing, most likely."

"It's because they don't like me. The Duchess has made sure of it. That's okay, I don't like them, either."

"Like I said, it's probably Wonderland nonsense! Personally, I have never seen the wisdom in trying to fit into a place I don't belong or trying to please people who don't like me. And I feel foolish and ashamed for encouraging you to do so. I think it's time we find a way to leave this place."

"Do you really mean it?"

"I do! I promise, if there is a way out of here, I will find it."

With this declaration, the Queen seemed more like herself. Less dispirited. More alive with curiosity and hope. Inspired by purpose and plans for the future. And things had been good again for a time, until the morning the White Queen's letter arrived.

The Queen shook with anger as she read the letter.

"This will not stand, Rabbit. There is no way I will let this overblown chess piece take you away! How does she justify charging you for a crime you have not yet committed?"

"Time works differently for the White Queen."

"Wonderland nonsense! This White Queen thinks she can march her guards into my castle and take away my dearest friend? Well, if she tries, she will have a war on her hands. I will not stand for it! I will have them slaughtered where they stand before I see that happen."

"Your Majesty!"

A Letter from the White Queen

"Don't *Your Majesty* me, Rabbit! Enough is enough! I will have her head!"

"Her head, Your Majesty?"

"Her head, Rabbit!"

"I'm not sure it will come to all that, Your Majesty. Perhaps I should just visit the White Queen myself, and see what this is all about."

"No, Rabbit, she will come here to my castle and face me. You are not to venture anywhere near her castle. Tell the guards to go fetch her immediately and bring her here to me!"

"But what if she refuses?"

"Then off with her head! Ready the pikes, Rabbit!"

"The pikes, Your Majesty?"

"Yes, the pikes! Don't you recall my orders for the smithy to make us some sturdy pikes? For all we know, the White Queen has a gigantic head like the Duchess!"

"I thought that was a joke, Your Majesty."

"I would never joke about beheading someone, Rabbit."

Within moments, there was a knock at the door. It was one of the pages with another letter from the White Queen. The Queen of Hearts snatched it from the silver tray and opened it without bothering to use her letter opener.

"It appears we are *both* to be arrested," said the Queen, flinging the letter into the air.

"What? May I see the letter, Your Majesty?"

"Be my guest! Maybe you can make more sense of it than I."

"It says you are to be arrested for killing everyone in Wonderland!"

"That's a silly notion, Rabbit. Where would she get an idea like that?"

"She does see the future, Your Majesty. She says you are going to behead everyone."

"Are you saying I would do such a thing? Behead everyone in Wonderland?"

"You just said you would behead the White Queen, and you've threatened to behead the Duchess on several occasions."

"And I shall, if she persists in this lunacy! Am I

A Letter from the White Queen

not the Queen of Wonderland? Does no one in this upside-down place take me seriously? Do they take anything seriously?"

"I don't think there is much anyone here takes seriously, Your Majesty."

"Well, they are going to start taking me seriously when I start chopping off their heads!" she said.

"I daresay they won't be doing much of anything without heads, Your Majesty."

"Oh, you know what I meant, Rabbit."

"Yes, Your Majesty, I'm afraid I do."

Chapter IX

The White Rabbit's Blunder

The Queen of Hearts was in the hedge maze when the White Rabbit came upon her. It had been some days since they received their letters from the White Queen, and the Queen of Hearts was standing in almost the exact spot he had found her on their first day, except this time she wasn't toppling over the tall hedge while trying to climb it. She knew her friend was standing there, watching her as she stood perfectly still and quietly contemplating which path to take in the maze. She did this often as of late, wandering the maze on her own, enjoying the solitude

The White Rabbit's Blunder

and serenity. That was likely why the rabbit hadn't made his salutations. He knew better than anyone how dear the quiet had become for her. She couldn't stand any sort of noise or vexations. And the only places she found peace were in her bedchambers and in the hedge maze.

"Rabbit, tell the groundskeepers I want all these hedges replaced with rosebush hedges. Red rosebushes, not yellow, not pink, not purple, and for goodness' sake, not white. I detest white roses. I want red rosebushes, make that clear," she said without turning around to see if he was actually there. She knew he was there. She could feel him. She always knew when her most trusted friend, her only friend, was nearby.

"Of course, Your Majesty. But where will you take your walks in the meantime? You've remarked more than once that this is one of your only respites. Perhaps we can just plant more red rosebushes outside the maze?"

"You have a good point, Rabbit. And as it is one

of the only places I can be alone, I shall take your advice, and we shall make it one of the most glorious places in my kingdom."

"Indeed. And perhaps in the center of the maze there should be a place for your repose, a gazebo where you may sit and have your tea, and play cards."

"That's a fine idea, but how would the maids ever find me in order to serve?"

"I will bring it, Your Majesty."

"And sometimes join me, I hope?"

"That would be most agreeable, Your Majesty."

"Rabbit, as much as I enjoy planning gardens with you, I assume you're here for a reason. Tell me, what new version of torment is upon us now?"

"Is it that obvious?"

"Your ears and whiskers are twitching, Rabbit."

"Indeed. Let me get right to it, then. You recall the letters we received from the White Queen?"

"Indeed, Rabbit, how could I forget? I have been doing little else but formulating my plans to invade her castle."

"Well, it would seem we are not the only

The White Rabbit's Blunder

individuals with arrest warrants issued by the White Queen. The hatter received one just this morning for some crime or another he has yet to commit. And this isn't the first time he has been arrested for something he was accused of doing in the future."

"I see. And by what authority does this White Queen issue such warrants and sentences, may I ask? Of course, it would be redundant to say this place is utterly befuddling, but I can't make heads or tails of anything. Who is the ruler of this land? On my first day you said I was the Queen, and then I come to find out there is a White Queen, who, by all accounts, is nothing more than a walking chess piece, so therefore not an actual monarch, but nevertheless conducts herself as if she is the ruler of Wonderland. And apparently we have a Red Queen who is in possession of the dragon that ate my servants and who, by the way, has never bothered to make her apologies or even introduce herself to me. For all I know, Wonderland is littered with demented kings and queens, all thinking they are the true rulers of Wonderland. So what is it, Rabbit? Are we all the rulers of Wonderland? Do we only rule our corners of this place? Would it even matter if we actually found a way out of Wonderland and left it behind us, as we have so often wished?"

"If you left, two terrible things would happen, Your Majesty, the lesser of which would be leaving me behind."

"The lesser of which? I would never leave you behind, Rabbit. How could you think such a thing? I thought we agreed to leave this place together."

"We did. And I would. But I've come to realize if we left, things wouldn't be the same, Your Majesty. I would be just an ordinary rabbit."

"How do you know this, Rabbit? What have you found?"

"It's just a feeling, Your Majesty."

The White Rabbit hated keeping things from the Queen, but he wasn't ready to tell her he had been searching for ways out of Wonderland since shortly after his declaration they should leave. That he had in fact already found a way out of Wonderland, through a rabbit hole, of all places. He felt terrible keeping this from the Queen because he knew how much she wanted to escape, but he wasn't sure the land the rabbit hole led him to was the right place for either of them.

On the first occasion he went through the rabbit hole and visited this new land, and there had been several visits since, he actually quite liked it. But he soon realized, once he traversed the magical passageway, he was much smaller than he was while in Wonderland; in fact, he was, he supposed, the size of an ordinary rabbit, that is to say *a rabbit of usual size*, and to make matters worse, no one in this new land seemed to understand him when he spoke to them.

In every other way, London, as he soon learned was this land's name, was an exceedingly lovely place, all green with colorful flowers and large trees to sleep under, with ladies prettily dressed in many colors and full skirts pushing prams with babies dressed in white lace who didn't scream, and gentlemen in top hats with walking sticks and morning coats. It was all very civilized. It was almost perfect. He could imagine his Queen there, happy and tranquil, conversing with ladies in the park, throwing dinner parties in a smart London flat, playing card games in her parlor, but he didn't see a place for himself in her life there, not as they were now.

On each of his visits he learned more about this strange place by listening to the people chatting on their walks, or reading the headlines on newspapers that were abandoned on park benches. It seemed this land was ruled by a tragic queen by the name of Victoria, who by all accounts was steadfastly in love with her prince. The people of this land were rather genteel, and far more reserved than those in Wonderland. It seemed to be the perfect place for them, really, except for a singular and insurmountable matter: London did not have talking animals. He wondered if *his* Queen of Hearts went through the rabbit hole, would she turn into one of these people who could not understand animals? The thought of it broke his heart, and so he kept searching. For all he knew, there were many rabbit holes throughout Wonderland that lead to other worlds, and perhaps he would find one that was perfectly suited to both

The White Rabbit's Blunder

of them. Until then he was going to keep his findings to himself and do what he could to keep his Queen happy and out of trouble.

He could tell the Queen suspected he was keeping something from her. He saw that glint in her eye when she was onto someone, but she said nothing more about it and went back to their conversation, for which he was thankful.

"What's the other terrible thing that would happen if I left Wonderland, Rabbit?" she said, bringing him out of his thoughts and back into the hedge maze with her.

"Everyone's fates would be in the hands of the Red and White Queens."

"You still mean for us to find a way out of here, don't you Rabbit? You haven't discovered we are trapped here as I feared and are keeping it from me?"

"Of course not, Your Majesty. Finding a way out together is my highest priority. I suppose I was just thinking what might happen after you've gone."

"You mean what might happen after we've both gone."

"Of course, Your Majesty. But what will they do without a ruler?"

"I think you're forgetting the King."

"Why not? *You* always do," he said, making them both bust out in laughter.

"But seriously, Rabbit, you have a good point. We can't leave until we know everyone will be left in good hands. Whether we stay or go, we have to kill the Red and White Queens. The Duchess, too, when I think of it. I cannot leave this place one day in the hands of a soothsayer arresting people on whims or a queen who cannot control her own dragon. And if we are forced to stay in this wretched place, if there is after all no escape, I will not abide sharing my rule with these dangerous queens! So, Rabbit, tell me, then: who should we kill first? I think it should be the White Queen, she is the immediate threat."

"Your Majesty, please! Shouldn't we first speak to the hatter? He seems to have the most experience with the White Queen, and he might have some advice to share, some insight."

"Oh yes, that's an excellent idea, Rabbit. That

The White Rabbit's Blunder

might give us an advantage when storming her castle. Though I was quite looking forward to chopping off her head in my own courtyard. I hate the idea of having to bring her head all the way back here to display on a pike. Maybe it won't be necessary to kill all three of them. Perhaps when the Red Queen and the Duchess see the White Queen's head at my castle gates, they will fall in line. But I do so love the idea of all three of their heads . . ."

"Your Majesty, no! That's not what I meant! I'd like to see if we can avoid any head chopping, if at all possible."

"That doesn't sound as fun."

"The hatter has been arrested by the White Queen several times and released rather quickly. He knows how all of this works. It could just be harmless Wonderland nonsense."

"Fine. We'll talk to the hatter. But if this plan of yours doesn't work, prepare yourself for war, Rabbit. Alert the guards! If we are venturing into madness, I want the protection of my guards!"

"How do you think it will look if we march

through Wonderland with the castle guards? I mean to have a friendly visit with the hatter. Perhaps bring him an unbirthday present. I want to talk with him, learn more about this place and its denizens."

"We tried that, Rabbit! Look where it got us! Besides, what makes you think we would be welcome at the hatter's tea table when he snubbed the invitation to join mine?"

"There is only one way to find out. And if you don't like his company, you can always chop off his head!" said the White Rabbit, making the Queen double over in laughter.

"Rabbit! You're making fun of me!"

"Indeed, Your Majesty."

"I love it! But be sure to pack the ax, just in case."

Chapter X

From the Book of Fairy Tales

A Trip to the Underworld

Now that we reside in the Underworld with Hades, we not only experience all time at once, but we can read the minds, hearts, and emotions of every person, in every time line, no matter if we are in their company or not. Think about that for a moment, what that actually means, and the power and responsibility that come along with that. We are not mere witches now but goddesses of the Underworld, and until Circe, Primrose, and Hazel are ready to take on the task of scribing the Book of Fairy Tales, you will remain in our company.

And so it falls upon us to share our daughter

Heartbroken

Circe's journey into the Underworld. And since we can see into her heart and mind, so shall you, as if she were sharing the story herself. And as everyone eventually learns: all roads lead to the Underworld, and that includes rabbit holes.

Circe took the long path to the Underworld. She'd learned of this path when Hades came to the Dead Woods and shared his story from the Book of Fairy Tales. Before she set out on her journey, she embraced Primrose, Hazel, and Jacob, wishing them well as they readied themselves for their own journey to meet up with Tulip. There were too many signs pointing to the possibility of disaster not to seek the advice of her mothers. Circe feared just one more strong magical shift could break the worlds beyond repair.

There were far too many things happening at once: the trouble with Grimhilde's old mirror, Tulip declaring war on the Beast King, and now the Jabberwock disappearing from the Dead Woods.

Something was happening, something much larger and more complex than Circe could see clearly without embracing all time at once. She saw only flashing images, glimmers of the destruction to come, and she was unable to piece them all together. She needed her mothers, and possibly Hades's help as well.

She couldn't help but wonder how things would have been if Hades hadn't come to the Many Kingdoms so many years ago when her mothers were still young, starting a chain of events that would affect everyone's fates. When she thought about it, if it weren't for Hades her mothers might not have caused so much terror, bloodshed, and misery. But then again, if it weren't for those events, Circe would not exist.

She wasn't sure how, but she had a feeling everything that was happening now in the Many Kingdoms, and the worlds beyond, was connected to the breaking of the worlds and the powerful magic Hades performed to rip Circe from the Place Between in order to make things right with her mothers. She feared that in changing their fates, he set another chain of events into motion that could do more harm than they could possibly comprehend. And if anyone knew what was really going on, it was her mothers. So that was why she took the long way to the Underworld to see them. Time to reflect, and to prepare herself for seeing them for the first time since Hades took them to the Underworld.

It was hard for Circe to picture her mothers happy, to think of them clearheaded and wise. It was especially difficult for her to trust them, even though she knew in her heart she could. But then again, her heart had lied to her before.

The truth was, Circe was exhausted. There had been no time to process or heal between one trauma to the next. She still had nightmares about what happened with her mothers before Hades took them down to the Underworld. It had all been so gruesome and heartbreaking before he intervened. Before he saved them all.

The only sleep Circe truly got was by magical intervention. A powerful enchantment that made her sleep, sending her to the dreamscape. But even there she was not free of the nightmares. She relived the horrors of seeing Ruby and Martha claw their way out of Lucinda's body as she howled in terror and pain, cursing Circe for combining them as one, cursing her for causing their torment and madness, moments before Hades spirited them away and made them whole again. In an instant they were happy, wise, and beautiful once more, no longer murderous, bloodthirsty witches but the witches they were always meant to be, with no trace of madness, no trace of the broken women they had been.

And yet, Circe was still afraid to see them. It was one thing to face her mothers in the magic mirror, it was another to see them in person. To embrace them, and trust them, and perhaps even allow herself to love them again. Circe knew she had to put all of this aside, because she knew at her core, she had to see her mothers and talk with them about what might be coming.

After saying goodbye to Primrose, Hazel, and Jacob, she stood in the main courtyard of the Dead Woods. She looked up at the solarium perched atop their mansion, wondering if she would ever see it again. It was the strangest feeling, as if she should say goodbye to it now. She felt similarly while making her way through the vast cemeteries and past the weeping angels. As she made her way to the catacombs on the other side of the Dead Woods, she wept for the skeletal army that had been awoken to fight this war of Tulip's. Before Tulip's call, Circe had had dreams of releasing the dead from their contract to serve the Queens of the Dead, to let them rest in peace, never again to be raised to fight another battle. And though they were not like Jacob, sparking with the same life or self-awareness, she still shed tears for them because they were not granted the peace they deserved.

She wasn't sure how much farther she had to walk until she found the entrance to the underground crypt where the previous Queens of the Dead were interred. She had never ventured to this part of the Dead Woods, and had only visited the crypt in her imagination when Hades shared his vivid memories of stumbling upon the site by mistake while exploring the catacombs beneath his fortress on the

Forbidden Mountain. She supposed the fortress was his again now that Maleficent was gone from the land of the living. But she couldn't let her heart linger on Maleficent for too long, else she would never stop crying.

All of the tragic beauties of the Book of Fairy Tales lingered in her mind this day, and she felt in her heart they all deserved better. She wanted so desperately to change their fates if she could. She saw happy endings for each of them so vividly in her mind that she was sure there was something she, Primrose, and Hazel could do.

She hadn't ever truly taken in the awesome sight of Bald Mountain before this day. It was on the farthest point of their kingdom, a great deal away from their mansion, grounds, gardens, and cemeteries, right at its border. She was embarrassed to admit she never knew it was there before she had recently spied it in the distance from the solarium; the beautiful ribbons of blue and green light danced in the sky, creating a silhouette of the mountain that must have been otherwise shielded in darkness and mist.

Heartbroken

It was strange, though, how its name came into her mind when she saw it that night, as if she had known about its existence, even though she couldn't recall how. She might have thought it had simply appeared out of the void, if it weren't for a feeling it had always been there.

She could feel the power of this place, something far more commanding than the queens who resided beneath it, and she wondered if this was one of the reasons Jacob urged her to read the entirety of the Book of Fairy Tales. She had a feeling it might be.

At the base of the mountain were stone steps that led under the staggeringly impressive eminence of the mountain, and she felt a change in temperature as she descended the stairs. She pulled her shawl tighter around her shoulders as the chill penetrated her bones.

There were times of late Circe couldn't remember when her life began, and which stories in the Book

From the Book of Fairy Tales

of Fairy Tales were hers or those of the original Circe. It was no wonder she was so fatigued by her life and her responsibilities. She felt as if she had already lived multiple lifetimes, and she wondered if other witches felt this way, especially Primrose and Hazel, who were also older than any of them could remember. It was no wonder the Odd Sisters were so ready for death, happy to reside in the Underworld. Being a witch was exhausting, no matter which path they chose.

As Circe walked into the chamber that housed the previous Queens of the Dead, part of her wondered if the chamber would shake with the wrath of the Wraith Queens. She expected them to appear as they had before, full of fury and rage, but Hades had seen to that with a bit of his magic, and the ladies of the Dead Woods at last had some peace. The chamber was just as Hades had described it.

As she stood in the center of the room looking at the visages of all the queens who came before, she imagined her own statue among them, serene and tranquil, ever watchful over her kingdom, and the thought gave her more peace than she expected. But she didn't linger in the queens' chamber for long; one day she would have her rest there, but, though exhausted, this would not be that day.

There was still so much for her to do. So much to discuss with her mothers. She ventured on through the catacombs feeling like a wraith herself, gliding past the changing masonry from one place of the dead to another, and she knew she would soon be crossing over to the catacombs under the Forbidden Mountain. She saw there were other pathways, which she suspected led to other places of the dead, but there was no time for exploring, no time to satisfy her curiosity.

She selfishly wished Snow White was still in her company; she would happily pour over the Book of Fairy Tales for anything that might give them insight into what might be happening. But then she remembered Hazel, and that was probably exactly what she was doing. She supposed she just missed Snow, missed her company and calming effect. Something about Snow White gave Circe life and made her feel as if everything would eventually be okay. Though she couldn't help but worry about Snow back in her own kingdom, soon Circe would be with her, and together they would discover the mystery of Grimhilde's mirror.

At last Circe was in the catacombs beneath Hades's and Maleficent's old fortress on the Forbidden Mountain. She recognized the change in masonry and soon came to the part of the catacombs where Hades had once kept Maleficent in dragon form so many years before. She crept up the stone steps to the dungeon throne room, feeling the vibrations of the castle to see if she could sense anyone, and to her surprise, she did feel a presence. She wasn't sure what it could be. She didn't sense danger, and wondered if it was just someone exploring the old, abandoned relic in hopes of seeing the ghosts of those who lingered there from before. It made Circe want to weep to see this old place, beautiful and woeful in its decay, covered in spiderwebs and dust.

And then something completely unexpected happened, something she would have never imagined: she saw something white flash by in her periphery.

Heartbroken

It was an extraordinarily large rabbit, walking on its hind legs. She had never seen anything like it in the Many Kingdoms. She had seen remarkable things in this kingdom, but never a rabbit such as this, and decided her eyes must have deceived her.

"Hello? Rabbit?" Circe quickened her pace, hoping she could catch up with the creature, who had hastily turned a corner.

"Oh!" Circe was taken aback to find she was right, and was now face-to-face with a rabbit of extraordinary size, almost her height, wearing a rather interesting-looking tweed suit and carrying an umbrella and a pocket watch.

"I'm sorry, miss, but I don't have time to dawdle. I am late."

"But who are you? You're not from this land."

"Indeed I'm not, but I am surprised to discover the people of this land can understand me. But you must forgive me, I really am quite late for a very important date. The Queen needs me."

"Which queen needs you?"

"The Queen of Hearts. I must find another land

From the Book of Fairy Tales

for us to live in or else she will go to war with the Red and White Queens."

"I have heard of the Red Queen, but I am afraid I am not familiar with the others. In fact, I am trying to locate her dragon, the Jabberwock."

"Oh, that's what started all of this, that damnable dragon! The Jabberwock attacked us when Her Majesty and I set out to deliver cakes on our first day to everyone in Wonderland, and ever since things have gone terribly wrong. I'm sorry, I haven't introduced myself, how remiss of me. I am the White Rabbit, but my friends call me Rabbit."

"A pleasure to meet you. I am Circe, Queen of the Dead Woods, Lady of Light."

"It's an honor to meet you, Queen Circe," said the rabbit, bowing.

"I wonder, what did you mean by *first day*?"

"Oh! That's simple—it was our first day. The first day we found ourselves in Wonderland. Almost no one in Wonderland remembers anything before their first day."

"Intriguing. Tell me, Rabbit, and this is very

important, how did you get from your land to mine?"

"Oh, through a rabbit hole. There are many such holes throughout Wonderland that lead to different worlds. Or at least I think there are. So far I have found only two." He glanced nervously at his watch before continuing. "I'm sorry, I wish I could stay and talk with you. I have so many questions, but I'm afraid if I don't go now things will go terribly wrong. I never leave my Queen on her own for too long for fear she might do something she will regret. But I would like to come back and speak with you soon— that is, if you don't mind. I am eager to discover if this would be a good land in which my Queen and I could live," he said, attempting to duck into a small passageway.

"I am sure we could come to some arrangement if this Queen of yours is as amiable as you. But I'm afraid you're too large to go in that hole, Rabbit. However did you come through in the first place?"

"Oh! With this!" He took a small bottle out of his pocket. "I almost forgot my shrinking potion!"

From the Book of Fairy Tales

"And how did you grow larger once on this side?" she asked with a smile.

"With a piece of the Caterpillar's mushroom, of course."

"I see. Well, it's quite fortuitous I found you here, Rabbit, because as it happens, I am looking for the Red Queen's Jabberwock. It seems it escaped my kingdom and is terrorizing yours. I mean to put an end to it. Is this Wonderland a friendly place? Would your Queen find a visit from me agreeable?"

"You would be most welcome, at least by my Queen, provided you do not vex her with riddles. Though I wouldn't worry, I can already tell you are more sensible than anyone in our land. Once through the rabbit hole, go straight to the Queen of Hearts's castle. It is the one surrounded by red rosebushes and an elaborate hedge maze, and remember this: speak to no one about your purpose on your way there."

"I shall see you soon, Rabbit! Now off with you. I'm sorry I've kept you so long. I hope everything will be okay with your Queen."

"Oh! Your Majesty. Shall I leave the shrinking potion here with you? You won't be able to enter the tunnel without it."

"I won't need it, Rabbit. I have magic of my own, but thank you."

"Oh! You're a witch! I didn't know witches actually existed. You must tell us more about yourself and your home when you come to visit. We are longing to leave Wonderland. You'll understand once you've been there."

"Wonderland sounds like an interesting place."

"You could say that, Your Majesty. Now I really must go. Feel free to keep the potion. It's too large for me to manage easily after I've taken it. I usually just leave them behind. Goodbye," he said, taking a sip and scampering off into the hole.

Circe laughed as she slipped the bottle into her pocket. There was something about the White Rabbit she liked. Perhaps it was his earnestness, she wasn't sure, but she was looking forward to seeing him again, and meeting this queen of his. She wasn't sure if the Many Kingdoms needed another queen,

From the Book of Fairy Tales

especially one that was planning to go to war against the queens in her own land, but something told her she had good reasons. But then again, Tulip had good reasons to go to war as well.

She sighed and walked back into the main throne room. The eternal fires of Hades still blazed within the pit before the stone throne, as it had in Hades's and Maleficent's times. She took a deep breath and walked into the flames, and within a moment she was standing before her mothers in the Underworld.

All three of them were standing there smiling as if they knew she was coming, which of course they did. The last thing Circe expected was to cry, but she couldn't help herself, seeing her mothers' beautiful faces, so happy, and so like the young witches Hades had described from his memories of them. It made her weep uncontrollably as she collapsed in their arms.

Chapter XI

From the Book of Fairy Tales

Sleeping Beauty

Circe had no idea how long she slept in the Underworld. She woke in a large ornately carved bed surrounded by soft cushions and pillows, and under a cozy velvet duvet. When her eyes focused, she remembered where she was. She sat up and leaned back on the stack of pillows that were propped up against the headboard, then saw that Pflanze was curled up at the end of her bed sleeping. Just then, one of her mothers came into the room, and Circe knew it was Lucinda.

"Good evening, my sleeping beauty. Did you rest well?"

From the Book of Fairy Tales

"Better than I have for ages. How long was I asleep?"

"It doesn't matter. You needed your rest. But look at you now, your light has returned," said Lucinda, sitting next to Circe on the bed. "Doesn't she look so much better, Pflanze?"

She does. Pflanze stood, stretched, and padded across the bed to curl up in Circe's lap, purring. *We were all so worried, but you seem well now. All you needed was rest*, said the cat, drifting back to sleep.

"Ruby and Martha were in a panic, of course, fretting and hovering, chattering away, so I had Hades take them on a walk to the river. They love welcoming new souls to the Underworld. They will be so happy to see you're awake and well again."

"How long have I been here, Mother?"

"That doesn't matter, dear. What matters is that you are yourself again. You're pushing yourself too hard, Circe. You're carrying too much, and you need our help. Events are unfolding that could be disastrous for all the worlds, not just the Many Kingdoms."

"I have felt something coming. That's why I'm

Heartbroken

here." Suddenly Circe remembered something from Hades's story, and it sent a panic through her.

"Wait! I didn't think—years are passing in the Many Kingdoms while I'm here. How could I have made such a huge mistake?"

"What are you talking about, dear?"

"When Hades was living in the Many Kingdoms he went back to his own world for only a matter days, and when he came back years had passed in the Many Kingdoms, everything changed. That's what started all of this, and I've done the same thing. How could I be so foolish?"

"Hades fixed that, dear. But there are time lines in which he didn't. Would you like to see what happened?"

"No! Wait? What do you mean *time lines*?"

"Circe, there are multiple versions of reality. Our choices matter, and when we make them, it changes our fates. There are time lines in which you were never born, and time lines in which my mother never split me into three. There are time lines in which Grimhilde defeated her father in the mirror on her own and never attempted to kill her daughter, and

From the Book of Fairy Tales

time lines in which Aurora turned into a dragon on her sixteenth birthday just like her mother. This is our time line. The only one that should matter to us."

"How am I just learning about this now?"

"I think there has always been a part of you that's known. But I haven't told you until now because I know you, my sweet daughter. Because it is in your nature to try to help everyone, and I knew it would break your heart to admit you can't. I need you to listen to me, please. Just content yourself that in other realities Cruella and Anita traveled the world together and Lady Tremaine never came to the Many Kingdoms, that Maleficent became a wish-granting fairy and James was welcomed to Neverland as a Lost Boy. You see these fates because they are real, making you want to change the fates in your own reality, and maybe you can for some of them. But there are some things you can't reverse, no matter how powerful you are, because doing so would cause irreparable harm. It is your calling to protect those you love *here* in this reality, and leave the others to their own fates."

Lucinda could see Circe struggling with this.

She could hear the protests and questions swirling in her mind.

"Listen, Circe, I know this is a lot to take in, but we don't have time to talk of other realities or debate if it's our duty to intervene. Perhaps one day, when *our worlds* are not at risk, we will sit and talk and plead our cases to each other. I know it's your instinct to want to help, but the only reason I told you was to make you understand why you see other possible fates so clearly. And I wanted to be honest with you. Now, my sweet girl, Ruby and Martha will be back soon, and there is so much more I want to show you before they start fussing over you. Will you do me a favor and save your questions and theories for another time, and trust me?"

"I don't think I have a choice. You're not the same. I can feel it. Maybe it sounds strange, but I almost miss you."

"My darling girl! I am still me! I'm not always so serious. Believe me, we're not so changed. When Ruby and Martha get back you will see. We're just not so angry anymore, we're . . ."

"The witches Hades knew before I was born."

From the Book of Fairy Tales

"Yes, my darling. Now, enough of all of this. As soon as Ruby and Martha walk in that door they'll be screeching, covering you in kisses, and fretting over you. I'm afraid they are still rather excitable. Not dangerous, mind you—well, not too dangerous, anyway—but eccentric, and lively. It's lovely, really. We have a lot of fun here, Circe."

"I'm happy to hear it."

"It breaks my heart to say it, but there is no time for any of this. I wish it were different . . . I've wanted this for so long. Now don't laugh, but Hades conjured more clothes for you than you could possibly wear on this visit once we told him you were coming. They're over there in the wardrobe. And someone will be in to draw you a bath. Find me when you're ready, and I will take you to the hall of mirrors. I think that is the best place to start. And remember your promise."

"What promise is that?"

"To trust me."

"I haven't promised that yet."

"Yes, you have. I felt it in your heart. Now take your bath and get ready. We don't have much time."

Chapter XII

From the Book of Fairy Tales

Back to the Old House

After she bathed and changed, Circe stepped out of her bedchamber and was struck by something completely unexpected. The old house. It was just sitting there in the vast corridor that connected the many halls in the Underworld fortress, as if it had always been there.

It was uncanny, seeing the house she grew up in with her mothers. Everything was the same, down to the smallest detail. The little white-picket fence and garden, Snow's apple tree in the side yard right outside the large round kitchen window. Even the stained-glass windows were the same. She just stood there, overwhelmed by so many memories washing over her. She wasn't sure if she wanted to go in. She wasn't sure if she wanted to feel like the person who once lived there for fear she would miss her too much.

"Ah. It seems the house sensed you missed home and came to you," Lucinda said, walking up behind her.

"I don't think I want to go in."

"We don't have time anyway, but isn't it lovely? It was Hades's idea. He made it for us." Lucinda wrapped her arms around Circe's waist from behind, hugging her tightly.

"Then this isn't our actual house? Where is it?"

"Resting, in the place of its creation. You can call it whenever you wish. It belongs to you now that we are no longer among the living."

"Are you sad that you're dead? Do you feel cheated out of the life you should have had?"

"No, my darling. We are having the life we always wanted. Well, not exactly *life*, but you know what I mean." Lucinda took Circe by the hand. "Now, come on. I wish we could go in, I wish we had more time together, but you need to get back to the Many Kingdoms as soon as you're able," she said, leading Circe to the hall of mirrors.

The hall of mirrors was exactly as one would expect. A vast, circular, and seemingly endless chamber of mirrors. Circe saw straight away that many of the mirrors were fractured, and in some the broken pieces were missing. But there was a particularly odd mirror with pieces that didn't seem to fit properly, like the mirror was comprised of other mirrors, creating an entirely new world. And in it she saw someone she knew.

"I know this rabbit!" Circe spied the White Rabbit and a regal-looking woman she assumed was the Queen of Hearts. They were walking down the castle steps and through some gardens. The Queen looked like a woman possessed, filled with purpose, and she could see the Queen and the rabbit were arguing about something.

"I should have never let you talk me into leaving my ax at home, Rabbit! I have a feeling we will need it!"

From the Book of Fairy Tales

"The last thing you need at an unbirthday party is an ax, Your Majesty," said the rabbit.

"I think it's exactly what we will need, Rabbit!"

"How do you know this rabbit? Where did you meet him?" Lucinda asked as she watched the pair through the mirror.

"I met him in the catacombs under Hades's old fortress. The Jabberwock and its mistress, the Red Queen, are missing from the Many Kingdoms, Mother. I came here for your help in finding them, and along the way I met this funny little rabbit, who said they're both in his land."

"Leave it to the Red Queen to end up in a place with talking rabbits," said Lucinda.

"He seemed like a very fine rabbit to me. He's looking for a new home for him and his Queen."

"How did he get into the Many Kingdoms?"

"He came through a rabbit hole. I said I would go there to help with the Jabberwock and meet the Queen of Hearts, why?"

"She must never leave Wonderland, Circe, not ever! You have to close off the rabbit hole that connects Wonderland and the Many Kingdoms and convince the rabbit to do the same with any others he might have found."

"Why is this so important? No more secrets, Mother. I want to know everything."

"We've been keeping an eye on the Queen of Hearts for some time now, ever since we discovered she was created by our rage and madness. When Hades broke the worlds, he created fractures in many worlds, and Wonderland is made up of those fractures. That's why nothing there makes sense—because it's made up of pieces that don't go together. Before she found herself in Wonderland, the Queen of Hearts was just a playing card. She has no memory of her life before because she didn't have a life until a sliver of London broke off and fused to the other pieces that created Wonderland."

"London! Where in London? How big was the piece?"

"Small. Just a deck of cards from a drawer in someone's drawing room. But if the worlds break again, more of London may break away and attach itself to Wonderland—or who knows where else."

"How did you discover the Queen of Hearts was created by your rage, though?"

"It was obvious. There was an entirely new world in the hall of mirrors, and residing within it was a woman with our fury. We recognized it at once. You can't live with something for so long without becoming intimately acquainted with it, my dear."

"And she remembers nothing of herself before her time in Wonderland? I sensed the White Rabbit has no memory from before he found himself there, either."

"I think the Queen of Hearts has vague memories, such as a playing card might have, at any rate. As for the rabbit, he once served the White Queen in another land, before a shard of that world fused to Wonderland. The White Queen sees the future, Circe, but everyone assumes she's mad."

"And what do you know of this Jabberwock? I think I should bring it back to the Dead Woods. I can't have a creature from my kingdom terrorizing other lands."

"The Jabberwock is where it belongs, Circe, with the Red Queen. Leave this be, my daughter. You can't help this Queen, or her rabbit."

"Don't be ridiculous, Mother, of course I am going to help them. You just told me this woman is filled with your rage, with your madness. We have to do something."

"We tried, Circe. Remember the cursed items in the curiosity shop? Cruella's earrings, Lady Tremaine's brooch, James's boot buckles?"

"Yes, of course I do. What of them?"

"There are more cursed objects. One of which is a pair of earrings meant for the Queen of Hearts."

"So you knew this would happen? You knew Hades would break the worlds and create Wonderland. You knew this poor woman would be afflicted by your madness?"

"We knew it was a possibility. Things are different now. Everything's changed. We've changed. We removed the curse from the earrings and enchanted them with a spell to help her! We even found a clever way to get them to her, but she refuses to wear them."

From the Book of Fairy Tales

"Then we have to do a spell to free her from your madness."

"Without it she would be nothing! That's all she is. She wouldn't exist without our madness," said Martha, who had just walked into the room.

"Surely that's not true, Martha. The Queen is kind to the White Rabbit. I think Wonderland has caused her to become so angry, not us," said Ruby, who followed Martha into the room.

"Then why is she constantly craving cake? I see her eating it all the time in the Wonderland mirror," Martha responded.

"Speaking of cake, has anyone arranged a cake for Circe's visit? It's not a proper visit without cake! Oh, I wish Hades was here. He is going to be so disappointed he had to miss you, but you know how much he enjoys his banquets with the newly arrived souls. He would have invited you to dinner of course, but then you would be bound to stay in the Underworld. But never mind all that. We are so happy to see you, Circe. You've made us so proud!" said Ruby, covering her in kisses.

Heartbroken

"Oh yes! Ruby is right, we need cake!" said Martha. "We have to celebrate! Look at you, Circe, you look so much better after your nap. We were worried about you, but Hades said you would be fine, and look, you are! Oh, this is just glorious. Our Circe is fine! Let's bring out the cake!"

"Sisters, I am afraid there is no time for cake, or parties, or even fawning over our daughter. You have to calm yourselves and pay attention to the subject at hand," said Lucinda.

"I've missed you all so much. And I love how much you love me." Circe was doing everything she could to keep herself from crying. She hadn't realized how much she missed her mothers. And it surprised her she even missed moments like this. "Mothers, are you sure we can't remove your anger from the Queen of Hearts? It has to be possible."

"Of course it's possible, but she would no longer exist. It would be like killing her. She would become a playing card again. Is it fair to give someone life and then take it away? We've debated this nightly,

From the Book of Fairy Tales

Circe, we've gone over every possibility, and there is no good solution. Especially if she refuses to wear the earrings."

"But look at her! She and the rabbit are searching for answers. And the rabbit knows about the portholes. Surely if she came to live in the Many Kingdoms she would be happier. Perhaps I could help her," said Circe.

"You would unleash our fury on the Many Kingdoms again. We can't do that after everything we've all been through, everything Hades did to bring us here. Would you put Snow White at further risk? Put everyone at risk? If you bring the Queen of Hearts to the Many Kingdoms, she will remember our grievances and think they are her own," said Lucinda. "Think about it, Circe, imagine the Queen of Hearts running around the Many Kingdoms encountering the likes of the Fairy Godmother or Nanny, or even Snow White. Our rage would spark within her like dragon fire. She wouldn't know why but she would hate them, and she would want them dead. She would be fueled by our old vendettas, taking vengeance for deeds long forgotten by us but now living with her."

"Instead, she wants to kill the White and Red Queens."

"At least she has good cause for that. Her own reasons, which have nothing to do with us."

"Still, I think I should go to Wonderland and talk her into wearing the earrings," said Circe.

"No, you are needed in the Many Kingdoms. Primrose, Hazel, and Jacob need you. They can't prevent this war alone. You have to talk to Tulip."

"I promised myself I would go to Snow White before joining the others. She wrote me saying there was something wrong with Grimhilde's old mirror, but I have not been able to get away until now," said Circe.

"Circe, there is no time for you to go to Snow White. We've seen what will happen if you go to war, and it will cause devastation throughout the Many Kingdoms and beyond. It will send a call to the other places of the dead, and it will awaken and bring monstrous creatures that do not belong in your realm. We have seen the coming of the demon of Bald Mountain, Circe. If he is released, all lands will be places of the dead. He has the power to wake the dead from every realm, and if he does so then all time lines and worlds will converge, and we will all be as mad as the Queen of Hearts."

"I felt this demon's power at Bald Mountain," said Circe.

"Where? In your dreams?" asked Lucinda sharply.

"No, on my way here. I went through the burial chamber of the Queens of the Dead and took the catacombs. Why, what's wrong?"

"Did it not occur to you the mountain hadn't been there before? This is something you should have told us at once, Circe."

"I'm sorry, I truly thought it had always been there. I thought you knew everything."

"Clearly not. And things have progressed much further than we realized. Circe, the time lines are already starting to converge in your mind. You can't tell the difference between our time line and other realities. No wonder you're so strained. Oh, this is very bad."

Circe had never seen her mother so panicked. Lucinda's hands were trembling as she pointed to the Dead Woods mirror. "There it is! A crack! A crack in the Dead Woods. Oh, how did we not see this before?"

"What does this mean?" Circe took a closer look at the mirror and saw the jagged piece of mirror that didn't look like it belonged.

It was Bald Mountain.

"Where are Jacob, Primrose, and Hazel?" asked Ruby.

"They are waking the rest of the dead, and will soon lead them to join Tulip." Circe was pale.

"How much of your army was awoken? How many stone creatures?"

"All of them, or nearly all. Why?"

"An army of the dead, of this size, may wake the demon. We have to stop this war, Circe. Oh, this is disastrous! This war must not happen, and the Queen of Hearts cannot enter the Many Kingdoms!"

From the Book of Fairy Tales

"I can't do all of this alone! I'm not strong enough. It's too much. I can't do it on my own. I can't stop this war, go to Wonderland, *and* help Snow White. She is desperate for my help, Mothers."

"Of course you are strong enough. But you don't have to be. We will help you, darling. We'll talk to the White Rabbit and see if he can persuade the Queen of Hearts to wear the earrings."

"But will the earrings help her? Will she be happy?"

"Only time will reveal that, but at least they will help control her rage."

"I think the best way to proceed is to be honest with the White Rabbit about all of this, and he can decide. Maybe the Queen of Hearts would be happier as a playing card again. Maybe she would have the peace she is craving. She is in misery," said Ruby, pointing to the Wonderland Mirror.

"Look! The White Queen has just sent out her guards to arrest the Queen of Hearts for beheading everyone in Wonderland."

"The White Rabbit should have never talked her out of confronting the White Queen," said Ruby. "I would kill her and everyone else in Wonderland if I were her," she added.

"Exactly. She is doing what *you* would do," said Circe.

"We've been recording the Queen of Hearts's story in the Book of Fairy Tales, and everyone in Wonderland is insufferable, Circe. Everyone except the White Rabbit, and the Queen of Hearts before Wonderland made her lose her wits. I'm not entirely sure it's our rage alone that's caused this. Any one of us, even you, would have been driven to murder in a place such as Wonderland," said Martha.

"Perhaps so. We all have murderous thoughts, Mothers, but we don't all act on them. I hope the Queen of Hearts doesn't, either, but with your bloodlust living within her, I'd say chances are she will. I think you should talk with her yourselves and not leave it to the White Rabbit, provided you think the earrings will actually work," said Circe.

"I think they will work, but it might be better coming from the White Rabbit. He should give her the choice. The Queen of Hearts might think it's just more Wonderland lunacy if we try to explain all of this. She might think we are just trying to trick her or something," said Lucinda.

"And if she refuses the earrings and chooses to exist, filled with rage?" asked Circe.

"The rabbit must talk her into wearing the earrings. Otherwise everyone in Wonderland will die," said Lucinda.

"And how will you get to Wonderland?" asked Circe.

"Through the looking glass, of course." Lucinda smiled. "Now give us a kiss, daughter. Tulip is still in the ancient forests, waking more trees. If you leave now you can speak with her before Jacob's army reaches her. Go straight to Tulip, my daughter. Leave Snow White and her mother's mirror to me. I promise Snow will be quite safe, my dear."

"Thank you, Mother, I will. Thank you for everything."

Chapter XIII

The Mad Hatter

The Queen of Hearts hadn't ventured farther than her own castle grounds since the day her servants were killed in Tulgey Woods. Wonderland looked exactly as it had on her first day, except there was a distinctive lack of annoying distractions lingering about the pathways or lurking in bushes or trees ready to pop out and vex her at every opportunity.

It was as if everyone in Wonderland decided to stay in their homes that day, or they had been spirited away by some magical wind, never to be seen again. If only that were the case. However refreshing it was to have Wonderland to herself and the

The Mad Hatter

White Rabbit, it was still a bit unsettling, seeing it so empty. It was the first time the Queen was able to appreciate Wonderland in all its splendor without its confounding denizens bumbling about, rambling off their riddles and nonsensical stories, and it gave her a greater appreciation for the whimsical beauty of the place. She had forgotten how colorful the flowers were, and the abundance of butterflies that danced on their petals. She marveled at the tall mushrooms, and ornately sculpted topiaries, and the distinctive streaks of blue and pink that dominated the sky at this time of day. She was surprised by how much beauty Wonderland held, and was disarmed by how it captivated her.

"Where can everyone be? I wonder if we will even find the hatter at home."

"He's always at home, Your Majesty. Even today." The Queen knew at once it was the voice of the Cheshire Cat. And, predictable as ever, he materialized on the branch of a nearby tree flashing his signature smile that the Queen had grown to despise.

"Oh, it's you," she said, narrowing her eyes at the

cat. "Do you do anything other than lie about and cause chaos?"

"What did I do to deserve such a greeting?" asked the cat slowly, blinking its large eyes at her and smiling.

"What did you do, indeed! You know very well, Cat! You gave me no warning your duchess was out of her mind, having her cook pepper everything in sight and insisting her pig is a baby."

"To be fair, sometimes the baby is a baby, and sometimes it is a pig."

"Wonderland nonsense!"

"That's a redundancy, superfluous, unnecessary."

"Cat! You're vexing me beyond words! What I find exceedingly unnecessary is this conversation."

"Clearly you're not beyond words, Your Majesty. You've just used a rather lot of them."

"Could you please tell me where everyone is today? You are the only being we've seen so far on this outing, and while it is rather delightful not to have to contend with the usual amount of Wonderland nonsense, it is rather disquieting."

The Mad Hatter

"Oh, that. It's the Red Queen's garden party. Absolutely everyone is invited. Well, *almost* everybody."

"Watch your mouth, Cat! Tell me, is the hatter at this party? And if not, where can I find him? In which direction does he live?"

"Walk down either of these paths and you will find madness, but the madness you are seeking is in that direction," said the cat, looking down the path that would presumably take them to the hatter's cottage.

"Yes, of course. I remember now. Rabbit mentioned we passed his garden on our first day. And you're sure he's home, then, not at the Red Queen's party?"

"Oh no, like you, he is not welcome. The Red Queen's guest list is very exclusive."

"Clearly! Thank you, Cat. Good day," she said, walking off without waiting for a response.

"That was delightfully abrupt," said the rabbit, his whiskers twitching in amusement.

"Oh, Rabbit. Haven't you learned? The less time we take to speak with the inhabitants of this wretched

Heartbroken

land, the less agitated we will become. Now, let's go!"

"You seem awfully agitated to me."

"And why shouldn't I be?" she said, stopping to make sure the Cheshire Cat was out of sight. "The nerve of the Red Queen, having a garden party and not inviting me! And why does everyone go to her parties and not mine?"

"Would you mind if I asked an impertinent question, Your Majesty?"

"Of course not! And since when do you need my permission to ask me anything?"

"Do you really mind that the inhabitants of Wonderland don't want to be your friends? Truly? They don't seem like your sort at all. Never mind they're unlike anyone you'd care to spend your time with."

"If I am going to be completely honest, it just all seems terribly unjust, them deciding who they think I am without getting to know me, all on the word of the Duchess. But you're right, Rabbit, they don't seem like the sort I'd associate with. I suppose I just felt I should make an effort because I am the Queen."

The Mad Hatter

"There is wisdom in that, my Queen, I just hate to see you needlessly upset over not being invited to a garden party that you'd loath attending."

"Too right, Rabbit. And it's lucky for us this hatter seems to have some sense, getting himself excluded from their haughty gatherings as well."

"I wouldn't count on the hatter having much sense, Your Majesty. He's called the *Mad* Hatter, after all."

"Of course he is," said the Queen with a great sigh.

At last they came to a wooden gate, through which they heard the distinctive sounds of jubilant voices rising in song. It sounded like "Happy Birthday," but the lyrics were nonsense. The Queen sighed. So much for this being different from the rest of Wonderland.

"Sounds like we're in the right place, Your Majesty."

"You think?" the Queen said, crossing her arms with a huff.

Heartbroken

"Come on, Your Majesty." The rabbit laughed as he pushed open the gate with his paw. "It's an unbirthday party, best be polite."

Once through the wooden gate, they went down the stone steps that led to a cobblestone path within a lush garden surrounded by topiaries, colorful flowers, and trees strung with paper lanterns. In the center of the garden was a long banquet table filled with numerous teapots and teacups that were trembling and bouncing upon the table. And at the head of the table was a queenly chair with a scalloped backrest, and yet no one sat in the place of honor. The source of the singing appeared to be the oddest duo the Queen had ever seen. It was an intolerable scene, what with the singing, chair swapping, and noisy teapots whistling and bubbling. It was all the Queen could do not to turn around and leave.

"I have no tolerance for this today. I can already tell this is going to be a waste of time, Rabbit. What sense will we get from them? Let's go."

"Are you still spiky about the Red Queen's party? I don't understand why," whispered the rabbit, giving

The Mad Hatter

her one of his famous looks as they stood back, watching the hatter and March Hare. They were so taken by their own company they didn't realize the Queen and rabbit had arrived.

"Your Majesty, I thought the idea of attending a tea with those biddies sounded intolerable, so why are you so upset?"

"Because the Red Queen never apologized! Her dragon ate my servants! I've been blaming myself since Tulgey Wood, and the only thing I'm to blame for is not confronting the Red Queen!"

"Shhh. Keep your voice down."

"Don't shush me, Rabbit. Remind me, why are we here? Clearly we will get no answers from these skylarking fools!"

"Shhh! You don't want to offend them!"

"Did you just shush me, Rabbit, right after I expressly forbade it? These fools wouldn't know an insult if it jumped out of a teapot and knocked them off their chairs."

"I assure you we would, Your Majesty," said the hatter. "I would invite you to join us, but there is no room at the table." The hatter wasn't at all what the Queen expected. He was an older man with a large nose, buckteeth, and tufts of wild white hair sticking out of the sides of a green top hat that matched his trousers. She couldn't take her eyes off his blue bow tie, which clashed with his mustard-brown jacket.

"No! No room! No room at all!" The protests came from the March Hare this time. His eyes were overly large and wild. He wore a baggy red jacket, a bow tie, and brown trousers.

"Nonsense, there is plenty of room!" said the rabbit, leading the Queen to the elaborate chair at the head of the table and pulling it out for her.

"But it's rude to join us uninvited!" The March Hare's eyebrows looked almost sinister as he pointed at the rabbit and Queen. It was hard to tell if he was serious or just having a lark.

"It's very, very rude indeed!" said the hatter. "Very, very, very, rude!"

"Remind me to get the hatter a thesaurus. This is past bearing, Rabbit. I didn't want to come here at all, but the fact that they won't allow us to join them

The Mad Hatter

is infuriating." The Queen threw her hands over her head as she paced along the cobblestones that flanked the long dining table, then stopped and looked the hatter in the eye.

"Now listen here, cuckoo, I am your Queen, and if I want to take tea with you, then I shall."

"No one likes our singing! That's why we aren't invited to the Red Queen's garden party! So, tell us, what doesn't she like about you?"

"Watch your attitude, Hatter, or I will have your head!" The Queen looked for her ax, then remembered the rabbit had talked her into leaving it at home. "Why are we here again, Rabbit? What form of insanity led us to this infernal bedlam? Tell me, because I can't recall why I agreed to subject myself to this nonsensical misery."

"Don't you remember, Your Majesty? You said you wanted to spend your unbirthday with the hatter and Hare," said the rabbit with a sly grin.

"What are you—" the Queen began, but stopped when she saw the hatter and hare's profound excitement. They were so elated they leaped from their seats, clapping their hands and running around the table lifting the lids off the teapots frantically, checking to see if they needed more hot water.

"Why didn't you tell us it was the Queen's unbirthday? Of course you're both welcome! What a coincidence, it's our unbirthdays as well!"

"It's not a coincidence at all! I daresay it's almost everyone's unbirthday today! Rabbit, this is maddening! We're leaving!"

"If it's really everyone's unbirthday, then why isn't everyone here?" The Dormouse's face looked truly perplexed as he popped his head out of a teapot to chime in. Of course the White Rabbit had told her all about the Dormouse, the little friend of the hatter and hare who often fell asleep in their teapots, so it wasn't a great surprise, but at this point a giant spider or crocodile could have jumped out of the teapot and she wouldn't have been fazed.

"We don't need everyone here to celebrate the Queen's unbirthday! Come on, let's sing!"

The hatter and Hare were singing so loudly about blowing out candles and making wishes, the Queen

The Mad Hatter

thought she was going mad. Between the teapots whistling and bouncing around the table, the clatter, banging, singing, and seat swapping, the Queen's head was swimming. Her chest was so tight she couldn't breathe. And the louder they sang, the faster her heart raced.

This was why she never went out, why she preferred to be alone, always in her room or the quiet of the hedge maze, because the moment she stepped out of her safe places, there was always too much noise. She couldn't hear herself think and it was hard to speak, her mind whirling with what she wanted to say, and no matter how politely she tried to say it, it always came out sounding rude. This, in turn, made her so angry she would scream or, worse, cry uncontrollably. Today, it would seem, would be a screaming day.

"SHUT UP BEFORE I GO MAD!" She didn't even recognize the voice that came out of her own mouth. She didn't know she was going to scream at them until she did, but it just burst out of her like thunder, frightening her as much as it frightened everyone else at the table.

"I think what the Queen of Hearts meant to say was that we came here today for a reason other than her unbirthday."

"Please stop talking about me as if I am not here, Rabbit! And stop telling them what I meant to say! I said exactly what I meant! Now listen, you exasperating, tea-drinking flibbertigibbets, we did not, in fact, come here to celebrate anything with you, not my unbirthday or anything else. We came here to see what you know about the White Queen, though now that we're here, I cannot fathom why. But since we seem to be prisoners of your mad tea party—a tea party, I might add, where the hosts have served us no tea, or cake—we might as well get your thoughts, such as they are, on this madwoman who calls herself the White Queen."

The hatter didn't seem to understand what the Queen was asking, and she could tell by the look on the rabbit's face he didn't want to speak for her for fear of angering her, so she rephrased her question.

"We understand the White Queen has punished you for crimes she predicted you would do in the future. Is this true?"

The Mad Hatter

"Oh yes! Many times."

"And did you go on to commit those crimes?" asked the Queen.

"Of course not!" said the hatter.

"Then why did you deserve the punishment? Oh, this is just more Wonderland nonsense!" The Queen slammed her fists on the table so hard, everyone jumped out of their seats. The Dormouse's teapot tipped over, causing the mouse to topple out of the pot.

"There is no use in trying to make sense out of nonsense, it will just drive you mad," said the hatter who was now looking at something behind the Queen as he spoke to her. What it was the Queen did not know or care. For all she knew it was some sort of dancing animal bent on vexing her.

"We have all come to accept this is just what the White Queen does. She arrests people for crimes she sees they will do in the future. Whether they do the crime or not is of little consequence because, you see, they have already suffered the consequences." said the hatter.

Something in that madness made sense to the Queen. They were paying the price for their crimes ahead of time.

"Then why didn't you commit the crime if you already paid the price?"

"Because I had time to think about it. I changed my mind. Maybe with time you will change your mind as well?" the hatter said with a strange smile as the Queen felt herself being yanked from her seat roughly.

"This is lunacy! Pure madness! It's incomprehensible pandemonium! Unhand me! I am the Queen of Hearts! I will not be queen-handled by walking chess pieces! I will have your head for this!" The Queen was flailing her arms and legs, kicking and punching the guards. "And unhand my rabbit! How dare you touch him?" she said as the guards dragged her, the hatter, and the rabbit out of the garden. "I *will* have everyone's heads for this! You mark my words!"

"That's exactly why you are under arrest!" said the guard. "By order of the White Queen!"

Chapter XIV

The White Queen's Dungeon

The White Rabbit hated being separated from the Queen. No matter how many times he asked about her or demanded to see her, no one would answer. He sat in silence within the White Queen's dungeon, wondering when someone would let him know what was going on. The dungeon was almost entirely dark, except for one candle, and he had been brought nothing since he arrived, not even a cup of tea. He hoped wherever they had taken the Queen of Hearts she was being treated better than he was. He shuddered to think how angry she was at that moment, the rage surging through her and the threats that must be spewing from her lips, no doubt doing nothing whatsoever to help her cause. If only the White Queen had put them in the same cell, he would be there to help calm her. And what would happen when they went on trial, would he be by her side so he could keep her from offending the White Queen? Oh, this was a disaster.

"You're a very kind rabbit. Our daughter, Circe, was right." The White Rabbit looked for the strange voice coming from the darkness, but it sounded as if it were far away, as if the darkness was another world.

"Who is there?" The rabbit squinted into the shadows, trying to see who was talking to him. And then he saw them, three shadows taking shape, swirling and shifting into something more distinct, three identical women with pitch-black hair and haunting eyes. He was so bewitched by these women, they were so different from Circe, yet somehow he knew they were the same. Witches.

"We've come on behalf of our daughter. She has a message for you, Little Rabbit. And we're afraid you have a hard choice to make. It's an enormous

The White Queen's Dungeon

responsibility for such a small rabbit," said the witch in the middle.

"I'm not so small," he replied, indignant. "Has she decided if my Queen and I can live in her land? Has she sent you here to let me know?"

"I'm afraid that won't be possible. It would be disastrous for the Many Kingdoms. It could cause all the other lands to shatter, and be destroyed."

"But why? Are you sure? I've visited two other lands and nothing of the sort happened. I know the Queen can be difficult, but I think if she were to get away from Wonderland, she could be herself again."

"Your Queen's rage will only increase with time, Rabbit. You've seen it happening. It's evident by the White Queen's prophecy. She will one day behead everyone in Wonderland unless you help her."

"I have been trying to help her. Why can't I bring her to one of these other worlds? I'm sure if we could just get away, everything would be okay."

"We've closed all the portholes except for the one that goes to London. And we know you don't want to take her there."

Heartbroken

"How do you know that?"

"We're witches, dear. We know things, especially about how magic works in nonmagical worlds. Circe wants you to know we have the power to remove the Queen of Hearts's rage." The rabbit's ears perked up.

"Then do it!" he cried in excitement. "Do it now!"

"Not so quick. If we do, then she will no longer exist. She would go back to her existence before she came to Wonderland. A playing card in a deck, tucked away in a dark drawer and only brought out for parties and family gatherings." said Lucinda.

"That's the choice? Killing her or watching her grow more miserable?" said the rabbit thumping his foot anxiously.

"There are always the earrings. The gold teardrop earrings from the King. We put an enchantment on them to keep her bloodshed in check." said Lucinda.

"Brilliant. We will keep her bloodlust in check. That will be useful. But what of her anger. Will she be happier? Will she be like the Queen I met on our first day?"

"Sometimes. Maybe? We don't know." said Lucinda.

"You're witches! Can't you try to do a spell that will make her happy again? Make her curious, and adventurous, make her the Queen I once knew? Please."

The rabbit could see he had said something that touched their hearts. Something in the words he chose meant something to them.

"Look into your heart, Little Rabbit. The Queen of Hearts has always been angry, since her first day in Wonderland. It's been you, and your friendship, helping her to control it. I wish we could help you more—our hearts break for you, truly. I wish there was a way to take her anger away without taking her existence. But that is literally all she is." said Lucinda with a sad, almost guilty look on her face.

"I refuse to believe that. She was so much more than her anger. She wasn't like this in the beginning."

"Are you sure, Rabbit? She became angry on her first day, and it's just gotten worse. And we know it's not her fault. The inhabitants of Wonderland are insufferable. They feed her rage by the day. Truthfully, I think she would be happier back in that drawing room drawer, where it's dark and quiet and there is no one to bother her, but that choice should be hers. Will you tell her, Rabbit? Will you give her the choice? Here." Lucinda handed the rabbit a small round pocket mirror.

"She feels her joy just as strongly. I have seen it," said the rabbit.

"And you have done an admirable job trying to steer her toward joy. She is very lucky to have you as a friend. Once you have her answer, call us in this magic looking glass, and we will respect her wishes either way, as long as she agrees to put on the earrings and promises never to take them off."

"I will talk to her."

"Very well. And don't grieve over not finding a new home in the Many Kingdoms. Even if it were a possibility for you and your Queen to live there, it will soon be ravaged by war. It's not a safe place, especially for little rabbits. There are creatures there even more dangerous than your Jabberwock."

"Do you hear that?" asked the rabbit, snapping his head in the other direction. "I think someone is coming."

"Yes, Little Rabbit, I'm afraid so, and they are coming for you," said Lucinda.

The White Rabbit blinked several times, wondering if he had imagined the three witches who had been there only moments before. Surely he *hadn't* imagined them; then again, he was starting to understand that almost anything was possible in Wonderland. He heard the jingling of keys and heavy footfalls coming toward him, so he stood up and braced himself for whatever came next, closing his eyes. When he opened them, he saw a lanky young man dressed entirely in white standing at his cell and holding a large metal ring that contained an enormous skeleton key.

"The White Queen is ready to see you now."

"Will the Queen of Hearts be there?"

Heartbroken

"This is your trial, White Rabbit, not the Queen of Hearts's."

The young man slipped the long skeleton key into the lock and turned it, opening the gate to the cell and motioning to the rabbit to come out.

"Come along, Rabbit, the White Queen is waiting for you."

"She is not my queen!" said the rabbit, giving the guard a dirty look.

"That remains to be seen."

The guard ushered the rabbit into the throne room. It had white marble walls and black-and-white checkered marble floors, with large white columns that soared to domed ceilings that revealed the clear night sky sparkling with stars. The Queen sat on a white velvet throne, dressed entirely in white. Her hair was frizzy, sticking out on either side of her enormous and awkward crown, which was ill-suited to her head. She had a frown on her face and lines under her eyes, as if she hardly slept. Her attire looked shabby, more like a bedsheet than royal robes, and she grasped at them as if she were cold. To the rabbit, she looked rather more disagreeable than the Queen of Hearts, and quite possibly more harried. The only decorations in the room were white roses in large marble vases placed around the perimeter. It was the most unremarkable space he had ever seen, and he couldn't wait to remark upon it over tea with the Queen of Hearts the moment they got out of there.

The guards marched the White Rabbit to the center of the room, a good distance away from the White Queen, who looked at him placidly.

"I demand to see my Queen!" he said, startled by the sonorous echoing of his voice throughout the cavernous hall.

"Silence! White Rabbit, you are accused of dereliction of duties to the crown."

"I have served the Queen of Hearts faithfully since my first day."

"I see. Then it's true, you have no memory of being in my court. I will not command you to return to me, White Rabbit, but I will remind you of the

Heartbroken

Queen of Hearts's future grievous misdeeds, and therefore it is my duty to warn you that you may one day end up on the chopping block yourself."

"You see into the future, is that right? Then you must be aware that if the Queen of Hearts does end up murdering everyone in Wonderland, it will be your doing."

"That's preposterous."

"Is it? You don't think this has anything to do with the Duchess whispering in your ear? She's turned you and the Red Queen against the Queen of Hearts. And what did she do to deserve that?"

"She treated the Duchess appallingly."

"How so? By not allowing her deranged cook to pepper the cakes? By defending me? The Duchess is the one who should be held for crimes committed, not the Queen of Hearts. She grabbed me by the scruff and threatened me."

"I do not punish for crimes that happened in the past. The past is the past, Rabbit."

"If that is so then why am I here? What is my

The White Queen's Dungeon

future crime that compelled you to drag me here?"

"Your complicity," said the White Queen. And the rabbit understood. Somehow he would play a part in this, but how he didn't know.

"If you and the other monarchs had just tried to be her friend, come to any of her gatherings, maybe this wouldn't be happening. For Wonderland's sake, the Red Queen's Jabberwock killed the Queen of Hearts's servants, and nothing was done about that! Not even an apology."

"The Queen of Hearts made it clear on her first day she had no intention of fitting in here in Wonderland. She woke up one day and found herself here, just like the rest of us, and instead of playing along and trying to fit in, she went her own way. And now she is paying the price. So what is your decision, Rabbit? Will you come back to my court, or will you stay loyal to the Queen of Hearts?"

"You know the future, why don't you tell me?"

"You may go, White Rabbit, but your Queen stays."

"Did you ever stop to think that this act, this incarceration, will be what tips her over the edge, the reason she will murder all of you?"

"It is the very reason, Rabbit."

"Then you admit it? Yet still you will punish her, pushing her to her future actions? Why are you doing this?"

"Because it is my duty to punish future crimes."

"The Queen of Hearts is right. You're all insane!"

"Insanity is in the eye of the beholder."

"Whatever that means!" said the rabbit, thumping his foot in anger. "So, may I see the Queen before I go?"

"You are in the presence of the queen, White Rabbit."

"The actual queen, the Queen of Wonderland, not some jumped-up chess piece playing at queen!"

"Watch your words, Rabbit. I could hold you in contempt."

"No, you can't. My contempt happened in the past. Now, may I see the Queen of Hearts?"

The White Queen's Dungeon

"You may not. Her crimes are so grievous she will not be allowed visitors."

"The King and I will not let this stand!"

"Remember, White Rabbit, I see the future. I will hold her as long as I like, and she will see no one while she resides in my dungeon."

"How long is her sentence?"

"Undetermined. The King shall receive word once it's decided. Now go, before I throw you in the dungeon again."

The rabbit didn't argue. There was no fighting against madness. The White Queen knew what she was doing by arresting the Queen of Hearts and putting her in isolation; she was going to drive her to commit the very crime she was being punished for. There was only one thing for the rabbit to do: gather the Queen of Hearts's forces and break her out of the White Queen's dungeon. It would seem the Queen of Hearts would have her way after all.

Chapter XV

Paint the Roses Red

The White Rabbit found the King to be as vexing and insufferable as the Queen had, and she spoke to him only when it was necessary. He now felt guilty for having tried to talk the Queen of Hearts into giving the King a chance, when it was abundantly clear they were completely different people, and entirely unsuitable. On the day the White Rabbit returned to the castle after being released from the White Queen's dungeon, it was exceedingly evident the King had none of his wife's spirit or bravery.

"Now, now, White Rabbit, I know you are very

fond of our Queen, but we can't go rushing headlong into a war, not when all of the other monarchs support the White Queen," said the King between the bites of food he was gobbling while at the dining table.

"Our Queen's Guard outnumbers the White Queen's, my King. And as far as I know, the Duchess and Red Queen have no guard. We have every chance of winning this scrimmage."

"Let's not forget the Jabberwock. The Red Queen does have the advantage there. I can't put any of our household at risk, you understand, and we shouldn't do anything to upset any of the other kings and queens."

"Queen Circe has promised to come for the Jabberwock and take it back to her lands. If she does so, then will you agree?"

"Who is this Queen Circe? What lands are you speaking of?"

"She is a witch from a place called the Many Kingdoms."

"A witch? There is no such thing as witches. Next

Heartbroken

you will say fairies exist! Come now, Mr. Rabbit, do you really expect me to believe you have befriended a witch and she will help you in this?"

The White Rabbit sighed and shook his head. "Your Majesty, please think about it. We live in a world full of stranger things than witches, or fairies, for that matter. Will you at least insist the White Queen let me see the Queen of Hearts?"

"Why would she let you see her when she won't even let her husband visit? Don't be such a foolish rabbit. Perhaps this will do our Queen some good. Maybe after spending some time in the White Queen's dungeon, she will be happy to be back at home again. Maybe she will . . ."

"Remember how much she loves you?"

"No need to be imprudent! That is none of your concern."

"If that *were* my concern, I should think the very best chance of making the Queen fall in love with you would be to break her out of that dungeon."

"Thankfully I am not as hotheaded and rash as either you or our Queen. What would it serve to have me jailed as well? I refuse to discuss this further, else the White Queen toss us both in her dungeon for colluding to overthrow her. Now please, leave me to my supper. I have had a very trying day, and I am desolate over my Queen's situation."

"Clearly!" said the rabbit, stomping his foot before leaving the dining hall.

It had been years since the Queen's imprisonment, and that initial conversation with the King. The White Rabbit had grown weary of living within the castle and moved out into a little cottage of his own, still visiting the castle daily to beg the King to invade the White Queen's castle so they could free the Queen of Hearts, but the King would always refuse to go to war.

It would seem no one but the White Rabbit missed the Queen of Hearts or worried for her state of mind in isolation. He wrote her daily, only to have his letters returned to him with the words *RETURN TO THE WHITE RABBIT, BY ORDERS OF THE WHITE QUEEN* scrawled across the envelope. Every day on his way from his cottage to the Court of

Heartbroken

Hearts, he would stop at the White Queen's castle gates and speak to the guards.

"May I see the Queen of Hearts today?" he would ask.

"You may not, White Rabbit. Not today, or any other. Not until the White Queen is ready to release her."

"And when will that be? The Queen of Hearts has been here for years! Years! For a crime she didn't commit. You have to let me talk to her. I have to see her."

But they would always refuse, no matter how earnestly the White Rabbit beseeched them. He felt like he was trapped in a nightmare, not being able to tell one day from the next because each day was the same. After he was turned away at the gate, he would make his way to the castle and appeal to the King of Hearts again, and when he said no, the White Rabbit sat at his desk and composed another letter to his Queen that he knew she would never receive. He did this every single day the Queen of Hearts was in the White Queen's dungeon.

Then one day, something was different. On this

day that was unlike all the others, he noticed as he passed through the Queen of Hearts's garden that the roses in her gardens and hedge maze were white. "Oh no! This will not do! This will not do at all. Who has authorized this?" The White Rabbit was seething as he walked the path leading to the castle steps flanked by white rosebushes. And to make matters worse, when he stepped into the morning room, the roses in there were also white.

Something wasn't right.

He found the King was sitting in his usual seat, which happened to have been the Queen's favorite chair, and far too large for him. It was their daily ritual, the rabbit and the King's, with the rabbit coming to the King to ask if he had changed his mind about confronting the White Queen while he sat there like a petulant child swinging his dangling feet, but this time the King seemed especially pleased with himself.

"White Rabbit, there you are. Right on time as usual. I have the most splendid news! The Queen will be released today."

Heartbroken

"Is that true? I just came from the White Queen's castle. Her guards said they wouldn't release her until the White Queen was ready."

"I suppose she's ready!"

"But why? Why now? What's changed?"

"Don't be silly. It's the roses, of course! I've changed them! She will love them. Don't you think it will be a delightful surprise?"

"A delightful surprise would have been attacking the White Queen's castle and breaking your Queen free of the dungeon! A delightful surprise would have been bringing her home where she belongs, rather than letting her rot in that damp dungeon! But I suppose roses will have to do. Oh, wait, they will not do, because the Queen prefers red roses! How could you make such a terrible blunder?" The rabbit at this point had long done away with any formalities when addressing the King and didn't bother to hide his contempt.

"The White Queen says white are my Queen's favorite now. She would know, Rabbit."

"Did it occur to you the White Queen was lying?"

Paint the Roses Red

The rabbit knew the King spent most of his time in oblivion, but this was on a completely new level. The White Rabbit always felt the King's one redeeming quality was his devotion to the Queen of Hearts; however, he had been calling that into question for quite some time now. In fact, he had been calling it into question from the moment the King first refused to do anything about the Queen of Hearts's arrest.

"And when did you have occasion to speak with the White Queen? Since when are you on friendly terms with her?" said the rabbit, thumping his foot in anger. The idea of the King of Hearts and the White Queen speaking together about roses or any other thing made the rabbit angry. It was a rare feeling for the White Rabbit, being angry, but he found himself experiencing it much more frequently having to deal with the King.

"If you must know, I am not, in fact, friendly with the White or Red Queens, nor am I friendly with the Duchess. They're all awful women. Locking up our Queen, spreading rumors about her, not inviting her to their garden parties. They're odious women.

How could you possibly think I am friendly with any of them?"

"Then why were you speaking with the White Queen about flowers? And how in Wonderland could you believe the Queen of Hearts prefers white roses now? Oh, this is a disaster! Everyone knows the Queen prefers red roses! How much time do we have to change everything? When will she arrive?"

"Any moment now," said the King, kicking his feet manically "Oh, this is so exciting! My dearest love will be at home with us where she belongs! She will be so happy! So pleased! So jubilant!"

The rabbit stopped listening to the King. He was far too panicked. There was no time. No time to change the roses, no time to arrange a feast, no time to bake the cakes, no time to welcome their Queen properly, no time, no time, no time.

As he stood there shaking and angry, a legion of servants had come into the room carrying bundles of white roses to present to the Queen upon her arrival. The White Rabbit quickly snatched as many of the bundles of roses as he could from the servants' hands, wondering why they were all just standing there like statues, as if frozen in time, with their eyes wide and seized by terror.

Then he realized. The Queen was home. She was there, at that very moment. And now he too was frozen in time, and with so many white roses in his paws he could hardly see over them. This was a disaster. This was all wrong. He had imagined this day for almost three years, and it was not supposed to be like this.

"Your Majesty, welcome home." The rabbit wanted so much to run to her, to give her a hug and tell her how much he missed her, but he just stood there feeling terrible he hadn't had the time to arrange a proper homecoming.

"What's all this then?" The Queen was looking around the room, scowling at the white roses. She looked rather disheveled, her once lovely velvet dress now threadbare, with patches of velvet missing, and the edges of her skirts were tattered as though the brocade that had once been there had been ripped away. The Queen's face was pale, frightfully so, and she had dark circles around her swollen eyes, which were red from crying. Her lips were chapped, and her hands looked painfully red, and her knuckles were bruised and covered in scabs that were cracked and bleeding.

"My Queen, what have they done to you?" asked the rabbit, his words catching in his throat.

"Again, I ask: What is all of this? Why are there white roses in my castle?"

"The King thought . . ."

"The King has never had a sensible thought in his head. This is my welcome? White roses? Didn't you tell him I hate white roses, Rabbit? And where were you? All those years and you didn't once come to see me, not once? I expected that from the King, but not you! I'm very disappointed in you, Rabbit!"

"I wanted to, Your Majesty! I tried!"

"Well, you didn't try hard enough. I'm going to my room. Tell the servants to remove all these disgusting flowers, and I will be ringing for some cake!" She turned on her heel and made to leave the room but seemed to think better of it. "No."

"No, Your Majesty?" asked the rabbit, trembling, waiting for her to turn around.

"No," she said, turning to face him. "I want *you* to clear away all of these flowers, Rabbit, and when you're done, I want you to march every servant who placed white flowers in my palace out to the courtyard and see to their execution!"

"But Your Majesty—!"

"Do not ever presume to disobey, or give me advice, again, Rabbit! Now, OFF WITH THEIR HEADS!"

Later that night when the Queen rang for her cake, the White Rabbit volunteered to take it to her himself. The entirety of the household staff was in hysterics and grief over the mass beheadings in the courtyard shortly after the Queen's return. He stood outside her door, too afraid to knock, afraid to see the disappointment in her face. Afraid of her condemnations. He searched everywhere for a red rose to put on her tray, but the King foolishly believed the

Heartbroken

White Queen when she suggested he rip out all the red roses and replace them with white. He wished he had never moved into his own cottage. If he had been here when the King ordered the roses to be changed, he could have stopped it. And he would have been there when the King received word the Queen was on her way home. He felt so much of this had been his fault. He shut his eyes and tried to close out the voice in his head condemning him for not listening to the Queen when she wanted to wage war on the White Queen before her arrest. Instead, he had talked her into seeing the hatter. If it weren't for him, the Queen would have never been arrested or spent all those years alone. And she would be wearing the earrings that the witches promised would save her life.

"Rabbit! I can hear you on the other side of the door! Stop that foot thumping and come in!" the Queen called from inside her room.

"Ah, I see you've brought me some cake," she said when he came into the room. "I hear you've taken a residence outside the castle. So, I was right; you have forsaken me. I never thought I'd see this day, Rabbit."

Paint the Roses Red

The Queen had bathed and changed her clothes. She looked more like herself than when she first arrived, but there was no joy within her.

"It's not true! I have not forsaken you. I have counted the days until your return."

"And how many days were those, Rabbit? How many days did I languish in the White Queen's dungeon, alone, and bewildered, wondering why my dearest friend had forsaken me?"

"I don't know, Your Majesty."

"You don't know what?"

"How many days."

"Then you weren't actually counting them. I see. Now we can add lies to your list of betrayals."

"I never betrayed you. Every day I asked the guards at the gate to see you, and every day I was turned away. I begged the King to invade the White Queen's castle, I told him to send the guards to bring you home, but he wouldn't listen to me. I even asked witches from the Underworld to help us! I tried everything!"

"Witches? Underworld? What are you on about,

Heartbroken

Rabbit? Have you gone as mad as everyone else here? If you say you tried to see me then I believe you, but I still say you didn't try hard enough. As for the King, he is a fool, and I expected nothing better from him. But from *you*, Rabbit, I expected more. I expected my dearest, most loyal friend, and YOU NEVER CAME! What has been going on around here? You moving out of the castle, and allowing WHITE ROSES IN MY GARDEN? White roses in my morning room? How could you let this happen? I can't even look at you."

"My Queen, I promise, I had nothing to do with the roses. I will have the groundskeepers fix it at once. And I promise you, I am as loyal as ever. It must have been terrible for you all these years. There wasn't a day I didn't think of you, wonder how you were doing, and wish you were back home."

"I don't wish to speak of it anymore, Rabbit. I never want it mentioned again. And I've decided I would no longer like us to be the same size. Make the proper adjustments before the next time I see you."

Paint the Roses Red

This broke the rabbit's heart. She no longer wanted them to be the same size. It took his breath away. The rabbit could see her confinement had been terrible for her. He could see something inside her had broken, and he worried there was nothing he could say or do to make things right. There was so much he wanted to tell her, he wanted to say he *had* actually counted the days at first but it became too painful, not knowing how long it would be until she was home. He wanted to tell her how he couldn't bear to be in the castle without her there, and that was the true reason he moved to the cottage. He wanted to tell her he had walked the hedge maze wishing she was there to quip with, that every day she was away was a misery and that's why he moved out of the castle. He moved there to be closer to her, not farther away. He hadn't abandoned her.

"You were my only friend here, Rabbit. The only person . . . creature . . . I could trust in this miserable, lonely place. You made it better, Rabbit, you made *me* better. But now, I am truly alone."

Heartbroken

"You're not alone, my Queen, I promise you. I will show you. Please give me a chance to prove you can trust me. Don't dismiss me."

"Oh, I am not going to dismiss you, Rabbit. I have plans for you. Now leave. And have all the white roses removed from my castle at once! I will see you in the morning room in one hour."

"But, Your Majesty, there is something very important we need to discuss." He put his paw in his pocket to feel if the earrings were still there. He had been carrying them with him all these years, waiting for the day when he could give them to her.

"I decide when something is important, Rabbit! Do as I say, or *off with your head*!"

Chapter XVI

The Garden Party

The White Rabbit returned from delivering all of the invitations to the Queen's party. He was nervous and out of breath from being chased by that horrible little Alice girl. She had been following him all day, and all he could think about was how late he would be to return to his Queen when all he wanted so desperately was to please her, even if she was no longer the woman he had known before she was taken into custody by the White Queen. No matter how he tried, the Queen of Hearts refused to speak with him privately so he could tell her about the Odd Sisters' offer of a choice—not that he expected her to believe him. At the very least, he had to try to get her to wear the earrings. But instead, she got it into her head to have this garden party, and he was sent out to deliver invitations. And since she invited everyone in the kingdom, it took him a very long time, not to mention having to contend with Alice, the precocious little house-destroying twit who chased him all through Wonderland, when all he longed to do was get back to the castle so he could talk some sense into the Queen of Hearts, though he feared it was much too late. He had, after all, just delivered the invitations to the Queen's head-chopping party.

The Odd Sisters had warned him he was under a ticking clock. That there could come a time when the earrings might not work. And as he stood there in the morning room, once again a rabbit of usual size and looking up at his Queen, he saw what those years in confinement had done to her, years with nothing but her anger to keep her company. Years without the witches' enchanted earrings to help her. It was too late. And it was all his fault. He could only hope that no one, not even in Wonderland, would be so foolish as to accept an invitation to their own demise.

And then, like magic, the most magnificent solution came to the rabbit's mind.

Alice!

She was on her way to the castle at that very moment. Surely she was almost there; she had been following him around the entire day while he rushed to deliver the invitations. Once that insipid little chatterbox arrived, the Queen would be too distracted. Too incensed by Alice's confounding questions and simpering little voice. Yes! Alice would distract her. Perhaps the Queen would be content to just behead Alice, and that would satisfy her bloodlust enough for one afternoon.

And as he stood before his queen nervous and out of breath, still angry with the blond little monster for the havoc she had been causing all over Wonderland, he decided the best thing to do was tell the Queen about Alice, the beastly little girl who had ruined his house and who was now grubbing her way through the hedge maze as they spoke.

Heartbroken

"Have you delivered the invitations, Rabbit? Every last one?" The Queen wouldn't even look at him. She was staring at the door, no doubt waiting for the servants to arrive with her cake. She had done nothing but eat cake and demand beheadings since she returned home. She was becoming more erratic by the moment and there was nothing he could say or do to calm her. He could see the Odd Sisters' hate like a tempest brewing inside her, and taking control. It was like watching a woman do battle with herself. He needed to find a way to speak with her alone, to make her listen, or at the very least devise a way to make her wear the earrings.

"Yes, my Queen, I delivered all of the invitations. All but one," he said, making her head turn in his direction.

"Which one? Who didn't receive their invitation?" the Queen snapped.

"The one for the little girl. I've come to understand her name is Alice, Your Majesty. She followed me all over. At first I thought she was my maid,

The Garden Party

Mary-Ann. But Mary-Ann would never grow to impossible heights and destroy my house, or scare the Dormouse, or confound the hatter and March Hare with riddles about ravens and writing desks."

"Stop this senseless chatter immediately, Rabbit! I refuse to listen to Wonderland nonsense!"

"Of course, Your Majesty. The point is, I didn't see an invitation for Alice with the others."

"Well, of course you didn't—she doesn't live here, you fool of a rabbit! Where in Wonderland would you deliver it? No matter, you make sure she finds her way here today. MAKE SURE THEY ALL DO."

"I daresay it might be a challenge to get *everyone* here with so little notice. Your subjects can be rather eccentric, and high-spirited—"

"And dead," she said startling him. "That is, they *will be dead* if they don't attend. It *won't* be like last time. Tell them without their heads there will be no more tomfoolery, leapfrogging, silly dances, or inane riddles. Tell them without their heads they will no longer be able to drink tea, or eat cake, or ask rude questions. Because, dear Rabbit, that will be the penalty for anyone who doesn't attend my party. Make sure they know."

I daresay that will be the penalty if they do attend, thought the rabbit.

"I believe it said so on the invitation, Your Majesty," he said. "Everyone in the kingdom is aware."

"Very well, very well, but will it make my nonsensical subjects attend? They must all come!" she yelled, her voice echoing. He wanted to reach out to her, to comfort her. He could see she was suffering, so overwhelmed with anger she was digging her nails into the palms of her hands, drawing blood. He could see the little droplets of red trickling onto the white tiles.

"They are, as you say, *eccentric*, Your Majesty," the rabbit said, casting down his eyes and wanting to hand her the kerchief from his pocket. But as he looked at this woman, he struggled to see something of his Queen within her. She just stood there, smoldering, trapped in her own thoughts, no doubt dreaming of everyone's heads on pikes.

The Garden Party

"She is almost here, my Queen," he said, trying to bring her out of her torment. Trying to make her focus on Alice.

"Who? Who is almost here? What are you talking about?" asked the Queen, twitching with anger and acting as if she was trying to clear her head.

"The little girl, my Queen. *Alice*. She is almost here."

"Of course! Yes! The little girl! Right. Well then, Rabbit, see to it the servants ready the croquet pitch and sharpen the royal ax!" She pushed past her tiny husband, almost knocking him over, which made the rabbit smile.

"And ready the flamingos! And round up the hedgehogs, and all the other nonsense one needs in this damnable place to play croquet. We will have our party in the garden! And little Alice will join us!" she said, throwing up her hands dramatically and continuing before he could reply. "Yes! A garden party! That's the perfect place."

"Oh yes, Your Majesty! The garden is the perfect place!" The rabbit grimaced as he thought about

Heartbroken

why she preferred to have the party outside.

"What do you know of perfect places for a garden party? *What do you know*, Little Rabbit?" she asked, narrowing her eyes at him. His Queen might be mad, but she could tell he knew what she was up to.

"Well, if one is going to have a garden party, the garden does seem like the perfect location," said the rabbit, eyeing her.

"Indeed!" she said as two servants came into the room with an enormous cake on a tea cart. It was the largest cake the rabbit had ever seen, big enough to fit four people the size of the King within.

"Too late! Too late! The cake has come too late! OFF WITH THEIR HEADS!" she said as she took a handful of cake, shoved it in her mouth, and flung the frosting from her fingers at the poor servants, who looked at her in horror.

"Oh, don't look at me like that. You know the penalty! Off with your heads!" She smiled as the guards came into the room to usher them off to the courtyard for their beheadings. The rabbit was horrified, and heartbroken to see how altered his Queen

The Garden Party

was after her ordeal. The situation felt hopeless. It felt dire. There had been a time when he pushed his Queen toward joy, but now, now he was hoping once Alice arrived at the castle, she would prove to be just as annoying and bothersome as she had been thus far that day, and the Queen would satisfy her bloodlust with the chopping of her head, but he knew in his heart this was folly. It was clear there was nothing that would truly satisfy that bloodlust now.

"Oh, and White Rabbit. I hope you don't think I neglected to invite *you* to my party. Though I daresay it hardly makes sense to have you deliver the invitation to yourself. So here." She took a white envelope from her pocket and handed it to him. He took it with shaking paws.

"It will be my . . . my . . . honor to attend, my Queen," he stammered, almost sure she intended to take his head as well. There was only one more thing he could think to do.

"And in honor of your homecoming and your upcoming, and no doubt magnificent, garden party, please allow me to bestow you with a gift." He took the little drawstring red velvet pouch that contained the earrings out of his pocket and handed it to her.

"Oh, Rabbit, you shouldn't have!" she said, taking the earrings out of the bag and putting them on at once. She ran around the room, stopping at each of the mirrors to admire herself. The rabbit eyed the King, who had been sitting there in uneasy silence, afraid he would recognize the earrings, but the Queen was dashing about the room so giddily the King didn't notice.

"Someone hand me a pocket mirror, quickly! I want to see them up close! And my fan! I need a fan. I can't host a garden party without my fan. Quickly, husband, go fetch it for me," she ordered, snatching the little hand mirror the rabbit produced from his pocket. It had been some time since he saw the Queen act this way. She was gazing at herself adoringly, and she was positively giddy. He liked this change in her mood, even if it was rather frenzied; she did for the moment seem distracted by a cheerful delirium rather than a bloodthirsty one.

The Garden Party

"Those earrings are perfect for you, Your Majesty! And your heart-shaped fan will be lovely with your dress. Good choice, Your Majesty!" he said as he watched her look at herself in the mirror.

"These earrings are divine, Rabbit, thank you! So demure, so cutesy. So me!" she said, spinning in circles. "Now grab your trumpet, Rabbit, and assemble the guards. I want to make a grand entrance when little Alice arrives! Be ready in five minutes."

She turned on her heel to leave, and he felt himself able to breathe. He had at last been able to give her the earrings. All he could hope was that he had given them to her in time.

But before the Queen left the room, she looked back at the rabbit and smiled at him over her shoulder.

"Oh, and, Rabbit, don't forget to bring my ax!"

Chapter XVII

From the Book of Fairy Tales

Mirror, Mirror

Lucinda stood in the hall of mirrors and searched for Grimhilde's vibrations among the many looking glasses. She discovered her in the land between the living and the dead. A land that was different for everyone, and of their own choosing. The Place Between, as it was called, was exactly that, the place between the land of the living and the land of the dead. One usually found themselves there before passing on to the other side. When the Odd Sisters and Circe had been there, they had conjured for themselves their old house, all of them happy, living together in harmony. For Grimhilde, it was a dark

From the Book of Fairy Tales

forest blackened by her hate, a reminder of the grief and pain she caused her daughter, Snow White. A land she chose for herself, where she could exist in perpetual grief and self-condemnation. Within this black forest there were many mirrors hanging from the trees, each of them reflecting her daughter's face, twisted in sorrow and heartbreak. Grimhilde could hear Snow White's soft cries and screams echoing throughout the forest, and they were breaking Grimhilde's heart.

When Grimhilde was still alive and first married to Snow White's father, Lucinda, Ruby, and Martha gifted her a magic mirror. This mirror was haunted by Grimhilde's father, a cruel and evil man who taunted and abused his daughter to the point of madness. He held his love just out of reach, to the point where she became obsessed with winning it. This set Grimhilde down a dark path that eventually led to her death, causing her to become the ghost in the magic mirror. Eventually she learned to travel to other mirrors; she became wrathful and possessive of Snow White, and the

Heartbroken

Odd Sisters had no choice other than to banish her. She became lost and wandering, unwilling to pass to the other side, endlessly searching for her daughter, Snow White.

When Lucinda found Grimhilde in the Place Between, she was hiding in the hollow of a blackened tree, shivering and cold. From the branches of the tree hung many mirrors of different shapes and sizes, and in each one she could see Snow White's face. Other than the haunting presence of her daughter, Grimhilde was alone.

Lucinda was taken aback by the grief and sadness that washed over her, seeing Grimhilde in this state. Seeing the pain in her eyes and how wracked with sorrow she had become. So Lucinda did something she did not know was possible until it happened: she stepped through the mirror into the Place Between and called out to Grimhilde. She saw Grimhilde flinch at the sound of her voice, and it broke Lucinda's heart to see her shrink back, too afraid to take her outstretched hand. The poor woman just buried her face in the crook of her arm and called out to Snow

White again and again, weeping uncontrollably, on the verge of collapse.

"Grimhilde, look at me. It's time for you to pass on. It's time to let your daughter go." Lucinda placed her hand gently on the woman's shoulder. Grimhilde's hair was long, tangled, and black, her eyes wide and darkened, and her face stricken with fear. Yet she was still the most beautiful woman Lucinda had ever seen. The fairest of all.

"Lucinda?"

"Yes, Grimhilde, it's me. I'm here to help you, as I should have done so many years ago."

"Where is my daughter? I won't let you harm her!" she said, shrinking away again, looking around frantically. "Run, Snow!" She screamed. "Run as fast as you can! Lucinda is here, she and her sisters have found us, and they're going to kill you!" Grimhilde stood, panic-stricken and cowering, her voice full of anguish. Lucinda could see the look of terror in Snow White's face reflected in the mirrors, horrified by her mother's screams. Horrified as she had been when she was a little girl, and afraid of the Odd Sisters.

Heartbroken

"Grimhilde stop! She can hear your voice through every mirror in your castle, and it's tormenting her, it's driving her mad. You need to leave this place. Snow doesn't need your protection anymore, not from us. We're here to protect her from *you*."

"From me! You're talking in riddles. You always have. This is one of your tricks."

"Look at me, Grimhilde. Really look at me. You know in your heart you can trust me," Lucinda said, and she saw something change in Grimhilde's face. She could tell Grimhilde knew she was telling the truth. She saw it in her eyes as they softened to her, and she felt it in her hand when she finally took Lucinda's hand in hers. Lucinda couldn't help but shed tears for this sad and broken woman, and for everything she had done to bring her to this place.

"Why help me now, after everything you've done?"

"Because I owe you at least that. Please, won't you let me show you the way to the other side? Won't you give yourself and your daughter peace?"

"But I can't leave her, Lucinda! I love her too much. She needs me."

"No, my friend, she needs you to let her go. You are causing her to go mad, just as your father did to you."

"Truly?"

"I am afraid so, dear girl. Come, it's time for you to cross over to the land of the dead. It's time for you to rest so your daughter might live. She will be fine, I promise you."

"But where will I go? What will it be like?" Grimhilde squeezed Lucinda's hand, fearful of what would happen next. Lucinda could see the dismay in the woman's eyes, the guilt for everything she had done to her daughter, but she also saw something else. Forgiveness. Lucinda didn't feel worthy of her forgiveness, but she was thankful for it. She hadn't realized until that moment how much she needed it, and what it meant to her.

"Oh, Grimhilde, it's different for all of us. I can give you whatever you wish," she said, not knowing it was within her power to do so before she spoke the words.

"I want to start over again. I want the chance to love Snow the way she deserved."

"Then that is how it shall be." Lucinda reached out her hand and spun it in a circular motion, creating a large arched doorway.

"How's this?" she said, smiling at Grimhilde, who stood marveling at the sun-drenched courtyard of her old castle.

"My little bird! Oh, Lucinda, is this real?" As they both looked through the magical doorway they saw Snow White as a little girl, sitting on the edge of the wishing well that was outside their old castle. She was listening to the sounds of bluebirds, and smiling. Snow was wearing the prettiest little red dress, and her hair glistened in the sun like raven's feathers. She was the exact image Grimhilde carried in her mind—her adorable little face, round cheeks, and sweet smile.

"It's real, Grimhilde, I promise you. Go to her, she's waiting for you."

"Wait! This is the day I broke my daughter's heart with news of her father's death! Why would you bring me here?"

"Grimhilde, listen to me, you're a powerful witch.

From the Book of Fairy Tales

More powerful than you realize, and this day can be whatever day you choose. You have a chance to do things differently now, my friend. You can live the life you deserve. The life you both deserve."

"But is this real, or magic?"

"It is magic, but that doesn't mean it's not real. I am giving you a gift, Grimhilde. Please take it," said Lucinda, smiling at the woman she now considered to be a friend while grieving the friendship they could have had so many years ago.

"Is that . . . ?" Grimhilde walked closer to the magical doorway, squinting at a person who joined Snow White and sat next to her at the well.

"Is that truly him?" asked Grimhilde. Lucinda had never seen her so happy, looking at Snow White and her father chatting in their old garden. She could feel the longing in Grimhilde's heart, how much she wanted to be with her family again.

"Yes, my dear. Now go to your family and be happy." Lucinda kissed Grimhilde on the cheek before ushering her through the magical doorway. She stood there a few moments longer, smiling at the three of them together again, seeing the pain and memories of her life before drifting away, forgetting everything that had come before that day until all that was left was bliss.

"Goodbye, my sweet friend. Live happily ever after." Lucinda waved as she closed the magical doorway with a flourish of her hand, then took a deep sigh. And when she turned around, she saw that the forest was no longer blackened, and the mirrors that hung in the trees were no longer filled with Snow White's face. It was now just a forest of mirrors. She hadn't expected to feel so thankful for Grimhilde's forgiveness, or so happy to give her this gift. But what was even more precious to her heart was how happy this was going to make Circe. This was exactly the sort of work Circe wanted to do, but it was becoming clear to Lucinda that it was up to her and her sisters to mend the lives they had destroyed.

When she stepped through the mirror that connected the Place Between and the Underworld, she found her sisters Ruby and Martha sitting on the floor weeping. This wasn't an unusual sight. Her sisters often cried. But this time, it was different. They weren't being petulant, or manic, or fretting over cake. They were touched by what they saw in the mirror.

"Lucinda! That was beautiful! You should have let us come with you!" Ruby's face was streaked with black tears and she was holding Martha, who wept so hard she could hardly speak.

"We didn't know we were giving happily ever afters! It's not fair, handing them out without us! No fair you getting all the credit!"

"I didn't know, either. I didn't even know it was within our power. It just sort of happened," said Lucinda. "We owed it to her, did we not? Why should we be among the few who get to spend the rest of time exactly as we would like?" said Lucinda, realizing maybe for the first time how lucky she was. "I just had a feeling Grimhilde was behind the problem with the mirror, and when I saw her there, saw the state she was in, I knew I had to help her to the other side, and only then would Snow White be free of her mother and Grimhilde would at last be at peace."

Heartbroken

"But how did you give her the happily ever after?" asked Ruby.

"I just thought how lovely it would be if she could go to the place where she would be happy. I looked into her heart and found her greatest desire, and manifested it for her. Of course there are others who deserve this, sisters. But there is no time to speak of it now. Have either of you heard from Circe?" she asked, scanning the mirrors that spanned the Many Kingdoms and hoping to get a glimpse of her. But what caught her eye was the Wonderland mirror. They saw the Queen of Hearts wearing the enchanted earrings, marching her way to her gardens to greet Alice, surrounded by guards.

"I see the rabbit was finally able to get her to wear the earrings," said Lucinda, scanning the mirrors again for Circe, but her sisters were still watching the events in Wonderland.

"For once, everything seems to be working out as it should. It looks like *everyone* is going to get their happily ever afters!" said Ruby, twirling in circles

From the Book of Fairy Tales

and laughing. "The Queen of Hearts is wearing her earrings, Grimhilde is with her family, and we are together with Hades!"

"I wonder." Lucinda studied the Queen. She recognized the anger in the Queen's face. She was familiar with her madness; it had once belonged to her.

"Who's been painting my roses red? Who's been painting my roses red? WHO?"

"What happened? Why aren't the earrings working?" cried Martha.

"It's too late. Too much time has passed. She was in the White Queen's dungeon for too long," said Lucinda. She wondered if she had done the right thing when the White Rabbit had asked for help, but she couldn't think of a way that wouldn't cause more mayhem. That wouldn't have caused death, confusion, and panic. She couldn't have broken her out of the dungeon without causing a war, and she couldn't bring the Queen of Hearts to the Many Kingdoms. Circe had decided on the plan, and Lucinda wanted to follow it. She wanted to prove to her daughter she

Heartbroken

could be trusted, but she couldn't help but feel she should have tried harder. And now it seemed the earrings wouldn't work.

"How is this possible, sister? It hasn't been more than a day, has it?" asked Ruby.

"Time works differently in all the realms, Martha. Why do I have to keep explaining this? Many years have passed in Wonderland—almost three, to be exact." Lucinda was doing her best to be patient with her sisters, but she found herself having trouble when she had to explain simple matters to them over and over again. But then again, she had almost forgotten this also, with her self-condemnations for not doing more.

"You said Hades fixed that. Where is he? Tell him to fix it! It's not fair. We promised Circe we would help the Queen of Hearts. We can't disappoint her!" Ruby was ripping at the hem of her dress, sobbing deeply, and choking on her tears.

"Yes, he did fix it, Ruby, but not in Wonderland, because Wonderland didn't exist at the time. Now, calm down and listen. The White Queen locked the Queen of Hearts away for many years because she was going to kill everyone in Wonderland, and the rabbit was unable to give her the earrings until she was released."

"She killed everyone? Oh, this is terrible! It's awful! It's all our fault," said Martha, who joined Ruby on the floor, the two of them weeping together.

"Well, technically this is all Hades's fault. He's the one who flung our hate into the universe, not caring where it landed," said Ruby through her tears.

"Calm down, both of you. Maybe the earrings will still help. She hasn't been wearing them for long, maybe they just need time to take effect," said Lucinda, helping both of her sisters back onto their feet. "She hasn't killed everyone *yet*. See, the Queen is playing some ridiculous game with that intolerable little girl, Alice. But everyone in Wonderland is on their way to her garden party, and she *will* kill them once they arrive. That's why the White Queen arrested her."

"Before she committed the crime?" asked both Ruby and Martha in unison.

"Yes, sisters, before she committed the crime."

"Well then, we don't see the problem," said Ruby and Martha, falling to the floor again, rolling in laughter.

"The problem is, dear sisters, as we have all discussed countless times before, the more the Queen gives in to her bloodlust, the more unbalanced she will become. She is living in misery, you know this, we've spoken of it several times. Why must I always have to remind you of everything?" asked Lucinda.

"I'm sorry, sister, of course we remember now. Please don't scold us," said Martha. "I think we were just so excited about Grimhilde having her happily ever after, and then it seemed like the Queen of Hearts would have hers as well, and I was thinking of how we could celebrate, and I thought perhaps it would be lovely to have some cake in the old house with Hades, like old times, but then you started talking about how it was too late for the Queen of Hearts, and I just got confused. Please don't be mad at me."

"I'm not angry, Martha. I understand," said

From the Book of Fairy Tales

Lucinda with a sigh. "Now please just stop crying. I need you both to pull yourselves together and help me. I don't know what to do. We promised Circe we wouldn't interfere beyond making sure she got the earrings and advising the rabbit to give her the choice. She made us promise not to remove our madness unless that was what the Queen of Hearts wanted, but look at her. She is going to kill everyone, and if that happens, it may cause more fractures," said Lucinda.

"Why didn't the White Rabbit give her the choice? I think it's because he is a selfish rabbit and doesn't want to lose her!" said Martha.

"He hasn't been able to talk with her about it, Martha, it's not his fault." Lucinda was rubbing her head. She was exhausted, and they were losing time. They needed to fix this situation with the Queen and do what they could to help Circe.

"But do you think the White Rabbit would have told her about the choice, given the chance?" asked Ruby.

"Honestly, I don't think so. He loves her too

Heartbroken

much. I saw it in his heart when we visited him in his cell," said Lucinda.

"Then he *is* a selfish rabbit!" said Ruby. "Look what he's doing! He's dangling that little girl in front of her like bait! He's trying to distract the Queen with Alice!" said Martha, pointing to the Wonderland mirror again.

"One less insufferable little girl in the world won't make a difference. Better her than all of Wonderland!" Ruby said as they watched the events in the Wonderland mirror, gasping when the Queen fell to the ground. There she was on the croquet pitch with her skirt over her head and her heart-patterned bloomers revealed for all to see. This, of course, caused Ruby and Martha to fall into another fit of laughter.

"Stop this laughing at once before I banish you to another room! I can't hear what is going on in Wonderland!" said Lucinda, struggling to figure out what the King was saying.

"Oh dear! Save the Queen!" The King was panicking, ordering the guards to surround the Queen to save her dignity. But Lucinda knew what was coming next. The Queen of Hearts almost immediately exploded her way from behind the guards, her face red and twisted in anger as she looked straight at Alice.

"Someone's head will roll for this! Yours! Off with her . . ."

Lucinda couldn't blame her; for all the Queen knew, it was Alice who was making a fool of her on her own croquet pitch, in her own garden, in front of all of her servants. She had only just come home, and already her court was encircled in a miasma of madness. Lucinda sighed, wondering if there was anything they could do to help the Queen, if there was any technicality or loophole that would allow them to interfere without disrupting the worlds further, and more importantly without disappointing Circe.

"She's going to kill Alice! She's going to do it! Look!" squealed Ruby as she watched the Queen of Hearts explode in anger.

"She should be killing that cat! He's the one who made a fool of her," Lucinda scoffed, wondering

Heartbroken

how much harm it would cause to reveal the cat's complicity.

"The cat started all of this! If he hadn't tricked the Queen into having his precious duchess to tea, none of this would have happened," said Martha. It was odd seeing how everything had played out for the Queen of Hearts, and even odder not being able to meddle, even if this time all Lucinda wanted to do was help. Even if this time she could be trusted to do the right thing.

She was brought out of her thoughts to find her sisters were still arguing about who to blame for the Queen's plight. When of course they knew who was to blame. Themselves.

"I think it's the Red Queen's fault. It was her dragon who killed the Queen's servants," said Ruby.

"I think it's the King's fault! Just look at him. Wait, what? The Queen ordered Alice's death, but he wants a trial? A *trial*? This is lunacy. Who is in charge here, anyway? If the Queen wants to lop off Alice's head, who is he to propose a trial?" said Ruby.

"The King, I suppose," said Martha, making Ruby laugh hysterically.

"I think the Queen is just humoring him and stringing out the tension for Alice! Oh, I like this Queen," said Ruby.

"Wait! I thought she was having a party! Where is everyone? So far, we've only seen Alice and that wretched cat," said Martha.

"Would you attend a party if you knew the host was planning to chop off your head?" asked Lucinda, unable to stop herself from laughing at the ill-conceived plan. Even the menagerie of Wonderland loons wasn't insane enough to line up to be beheaded.

"Of course we'd go to a head-chopping party, and we know you would, too! Don't tell me you're getting provincial on us, Lucinda!" said Ruby and Martha.

"Of course *I'd* want to go! I can only surmise the inhabitants of Wonderland have a very different idea of fun than we do," said Lucinda.

"But wouldn't it be just lovely for the Queen and us if everyone did show up? We'd have so many interesting characters to greet at the ferry this evening," said Ruby, making Lucinda roll her eyes and take a deep breath of frustration.

While it was true the Odd Sisters were free from their destructive anger and the deterioration of their minds, it would seem they had not lost all of their eccentricities or rather unconventional ways of looking at the world. Their moral compass was still, as some would say, rather tilted, but by no means were they the witches they were before Hades brought them to the Underworld. And if Lucinda was forced to be honest, she would have to admit her sisters were still a bit unhinged. It was to be expected, but nevertheless it was annoying for Lucinda, who was rather more levelheaded these days, even though she did still carry a spark of her former self within her.

"Sometimes I wonder if Hades really did take away all of our madness, sisters. Now, please, we have to keep focused on Wonderland." She looked on as the Queen of Hearts was leading a chase, now followed by everyone else in Wonderland, pursuing Alice down a rabbit hole.

From the Book of Fairy Tales

"How did this come to be? Why in Wonderland did everyone show up for this party—I would think her intentions were obvious. And what of the trial? Did they already have it? Oh, this is lunacy! Where is the rabbit? I don't see him! This is a nightmare!" said Lucinda, realizing she had let her sisters distract her from the goings-on in Wonderland too long. "Get the Book of Fairy Tales, right now!" Lucinda had a plan, and though she didn't have time to explain it to her sisters, she knew they would nevertheless insist she should. So to avoid the cavalcade of questions she knew would be coming otherwise, she decided to share her plan with them.

"We need to see into the Queen of Hearts's mind, sisters. We need to know if she's too far gone. I fear she went over the edge while she was in the White Queen's dungeon. We must know if the earrings will even help. We need to see if there is a point in the story when we can help her without disrupting the fates of others, without breaking the worlds even further."

"But what will Circe say?"

Heartbroken

"If we are able to help the Queen of Hearts without harming her or anyone else, she will be proud of us," said Lucinda. "Now get me that book," she added with a distinctive look she hoped would tell her sisters she would not suffer any more of their nonsense or questions.

"But we saw what happened at the croquet game!" Martha said. "The Queen was humiliated. Why do we need to see the trial? Clearly the Queen of Hearts found Alice guilty, else she wouldn't be chasing her down that rabbit hole, and everyone in Wonderland seems to concur! This is going exactly as the White Rabbit hoped. Alice is distracting the Queen of Hearts from going through with her plan to behead everyone in Wonderland. And we know her state of mind. Look at her! She is possessed by our anger, and if she catches up to Alice, she will have her head."

Lucinda was shocked by how much sense Martha was making. Perhaps she wasn't giving her sisters enough credit. Perhaps she needed to pay more attention when they spoke. But they still didn't seem to

From the Book of Fairy Tales

understand the full scope of what could happen.

"I agree with Martha."

"Of course you do, Ruby. You two always agree. But there is one thing you're not taking into consideration. How do we know the Queen of Hearts won't turn on everyone else once she chops off Alice's head? What if that act only ignites her bloodlust so powerfully, she won't ever recover? What will we do then? We have to see if there is a place in the time line when we can fix this. We have to see where her mind is, what she is thinking and feeling."

"Why go back in time? Let's just do it now. Surely if we had been able to do something to change the past events, we wouldn't be here watching the Queen and everyone else chase Alice down a rabbit hole. Clearly, the time to intervene is now," said Martha.

Lucinda blinked several times, trying to take in what her sister just said. It made perfect sense. The part she was struggling to understand was that her sisters who were usually nonsensical *were* making sense.

"You're right," said Lucinda, shocking both her

sisters. "Let's do the incantation now. Like the White Rabbit, we don't have time to spare."

The Odd Sisters stood, facing the Wonderland mirror, as Lucinda spoke the words of power.

"Through wind and darkness and from the farthest place, we join you now in an unlikely space. In a rabbit hole where you should not dwell, succumb to our distant and beseeching spell. Let us see into your heart, so that our worlds are not torn apart."

At once, the Queen of Hearts's face appeared in the Wonderland mirror, but this time the Odd Sisters felt everything she did. It was as if *they* were running after Alice in that rabbit hole, and they could hear the Queen's thoughts. She had been replaying events in her mind as she chased Alice through Wonderland and into the rabbit hole. Many of those who had shown up to her garden party had taken part in Alice's trial, and though in reality they had nothing of consequence to say, the Queen seemed to feel it was rather important. It seemed to the Odd Sisters the Queen of Hearts had succumbed not only to her bloodlust but to the nonsensical peculiarities of

From the Book of Fairy Tales

Wonderland. The Queen's head was a flurry of chaos buzzing with noise and chatter, vibrating with anxiety and anger. She kept replaying something Alice had said during the trial: "You're a fat, pompous, bad-tempered, old tyrant!" It was running on a loop in the Queen's mind, along with any other conceivable slight she had received. Her mind was equally plagued by terror, and trauma, following the events she had suffered since her first day in Wonderland. She replayed the morning she woke to find herself lying beside a stranger who claimed to be her husband and the night the Jabberwock ate her servants. It was as if she were experiencing it all over again; all the terror, confusion, and pain were as profound as if she were experiencing them for the first time. But the most dreadful, visceral, heartbreaking thoughts that flashed through her mind and heart were those of the unspeakable loneliness she felt while in the White Queen's dungeon. The Odd Sisters couldn't bear the pain seething through the Queen of Hearts as she remembered sitting alone in her cell, feeling heartbroken, abandoned, and forgotten. That was when she snapped. That was when she became lost and beyond hope. The Odd Sisters wept for the Queen of Hearts as she ran after Alice. But they knew she wasn't really running after the annoying little girl, she was running after herself, or perhaps away from herself. The Queen couldn't tell anymore. All she knew was the pain and horror. All she knew was the desire to kill, and to destroy everyone who had ever hurt her. Alice would be the first.

"You're right! She's going to kill everyone after she kills Alice!" said Ruby as they watched the Queen of Hearts chase Alice through the rabbit hole, heading straight to the door that would lead them to another world. Alice was struggling, trying to talk the doorknob into letting her through as the Queen got closer and closer, until at last, and of course at the very last moment, the doorknob let her open the door.

"Even the doorknobs are annoying in Wonderland! What an intolerable place," said Ruby. After Alice finally managed to open the door, she saw something rather peculiar: herself asleep under a tree.

"Oh gods, not *two* insufferable little twits. That's

From the Book of Fairy Tales

all we need." Suddenly, Lucinda heard something that distracted her from the Wonderland mirror—a small voice calling to them. A small desperate, familiar voice, pleading for their help.

"Hello, witches, are you there? Witches? Hello?"

"Who is that? Where's that voice coming from?" said Martha looking around the room to try to locate the voice.

"Witches! I need your help. Please. It's me, the White Rabbit."

"It's the White Rabbit! The White Rabbit! It's him!" squealed Ruby.

"Yes, Ruby, I can hear that, now shut up so I can hear him," said Lucinda, taking the small magic mirror from her pocket. His fear-stricken face looked back at her through the glass.

"Where are you, Rabbit? Why aren't you with the Queen of Hearts?"

"Everyone chased Alice after the trial and I got left behind. I don't know what to do. I can't find the Queen."

"She's in the rabbit hole chasing Alice!" Lucinda

Heartbroken

was struck with an idea; it jolted though her body like lightning. She wasn't sure what would happen or what the consequences might be, but at this point she was desperate to save the Queen from her misery, and this might be the way, without directly interfering with her magic.

"What will happen if she chases Alice into London? Is there anything you can do to stop her?" the White Rabbit asked.

"Maybe we shouldn't stop her," said Lucinda, eyeing her sisters with a knowing look.

"Oh! I hadn't thought of that," said Ruby, catching on to Lucinda's plan "But what will Circe think?"

"We're not using our magic. And we're not meddling. We're doing nothing," said Lucinda with a smile.

"Very interesting idea, sister. Yes, let her go to London. What could it hurt? As long as it's London," said Martha, with a knowing smile.

"Last time I went to London, I became an ordinary rabbit. What if the Queen and I can't talk to each other anymore? What if she doesn't know me?" asked the rabbit.

Lucinda felt bad for the poor little beast. She didn't want him to lose his best friend. She couldn't blame him. But she could see no other option; the Queen of Hearts had to go through the rabbit hole. She had to get out of Wonderland, otherwise she would kill everyone there. Her bloodlust was out of control, and Lucinda could feel the Queen's hate growing inside of the poor woman, eating away at her. Perhaps in a new land, things would be different. At least it wasn't the Many Kingdoms. Perhaps it would be okay if she went to London. She didn't know.

"We will have to deal with the consequences once they present themselves, Little Rabbit. Let her go through," said Lucinda, smiling weakly at the trembling rabbit.

"I'm afraid," said the rabbit from the small round mirror, but something flashed in one of the other mirrors, catching the Odd Sisters' attention. Streams of green and blue lit up the dark sky over the Dead

Heartbroken

Woods, dancing and moving behind Bald Mountain. And then they saw it, the demon of Bald Mountain, Chernobog, opening his eyes. He stretched out his enormous wings, casting darkness over the Many Kingdoms.

The Odd Sisters were seized with terror. Unable to move. Afraid for their daughter Circe. For everyone in the Many Kingdoms

"We know, Little Rabbit. We're all afraid."

And then, without warning, the mirror went black. He could hear the screams of the witches as the mirror cracked and the earth beneath him shook.

Chapter XVIII

Down the Rabbit Hole

The White Rabbit didn't have time to wonder why the witches were so afraid, why their eyes were filled with terror. Or why he could still hear their screams even after the mirror went black. The earth had stopped shaking, and he had no time to worry about witches or wonder why Wonderland had been trembling. He needed to get to his Queen before she wandered off somewhere and became lost in London. He needed to protect her. He had failed her once before, and he was determined not to do it again. He ran as fast as he could through the hedge maze and into the woods, passing the Tweedle brothers, and the

Heartbroken

March Hare and Hatter, who looked as if they were making their way home again. He didn't stop to talk to any of them, not the Caterpillar, and certainly not the Cheshire Cat. But he did stop to talk to the King, who was sitting on a log at the edge of the rabbit hole, his face buried in his hands.

"She's gone! She's gone! Whatever will I do without our Queen?" The King was blubbering uncontrollably, making a spectacle of himself. That is, he would be, if anyone else were there. The rabbit supposed he should feel bad for the King, but the truth was he didn't. He couldn't bring himself to feel sorry for the man who refused to save his Queen. The man who allowed his Queen to waste away in the White Queen's cell for all those years.

"I suppose you will do what you did all those many years she was locked away," said the rabbit, his hands on his hips and his chin high. "You could have saved her, you know. You could have stood up to the White Queen, but instead you let her wither, let her think we didn't care for her. This is your fault!"

Down the Rabbit Hole

"At least we knew where she was! This time, she just vanished! She's gone. She's gone forever."

"Vanished? What do you mean?"

"She disappeared when she ran through the door after Alice! Just like that! Gone!"

"Are you sure?"

"Quite sure. Oh, this is the saddest day. The worst of days. My dearest love is gone!" The King slumped over in anguish. The rabbit sighed. There was no sense in being cruel to this sad man. The rabbit supposed the King likely couldn't help but to be a fool. It seemed like many of those who lived in Wonderland couldn't help their demeanors. But the last thing he wanted was for the King to follow him through the rabbit hole. He would have enough on his hands trying to find the Queen on his own. So he decided to be gentle with the King to get him out of the way.

"There there, Little King. You go back to the castle, and I will look into this. Just leave it to me." He gave a great sigh as he watched the King make his way down the path to the castle. It seemed impossible that the Queen would simply vanish, just like that moment when she walked through the rabbit hole door. The King had to be mistaken. But he told himself to be prepared for whatever might happen as he made his way to the door, afraid of what he might find on the other side. Afraid to become an ordinary rabbit in such a strange and unfamiliar world. But he didn't have a choice; he had to find his Queen.

Suddenly, he was plagued with questions. What if the Queen wasn't in the park? What if she found London frightening and ran away? And how was he going to find her once he became an ordinary rabbit? None of it mattered. He screwed up his courage, remembering what the witches had said. That everyone was afraid. So he put his paw on the knob, opened the door, and stepped through.

On the grass right on the other side of the door was a playing card, the Queen of Hearts. But he knew it wasn't an ordinary card, it was *his Queen*. He sat there in the grass, just an ordinary rabbit looking at an ordinary playing card. If anyone in the park had noticed, they would think he once belonged to a magician. They would never guess he was from another world, a rabbit who failed his Queen.

He was heartbroken. He hated that she no longer trusted him, that she didn't consider him to be her friend. And just like that, before he could prove he hadn't betrayed her, she was gone. Gone forever, without knowing how much he truly loved her. What would he do in Wonderland now without the Queen? His dearest and only friend.

He picked up the card with his mouth and hopped through the door back to Wonderland, and once he was on the other side, he was no longer an ordinary rabbit, and the card was no longer an ordinary playing card but his Queen. He couldn't believe it. She looked just as she had on their first day.

"My Queen! You're alive!" he said wrapping his furry arms around her, hugging her over and over in joy and disbelief.

"Well, of course I'm alive! But how is it that I find myself being hugged by a talking rabbit wearing a silly ruff around his neck and carrying a trumpet? It

Heartbroken

is odd, don't you think? But I suppose I don't know what is odd and what is ordinary, considering I have no idea who I am or what this place is," added the Queen, making the rabbit laugh.

"It doesn't matter who you were, Your Majesty, what matters is who you are today." He smiled at her. "Today is your first day," said the rabbit, trying not to cry.

"What do you mean, *first day?*"

"Everyone's story has to start somewhere, doesn't it? And it seems our story starts today, here, right outside this rabbit hole. Why not make the most of it?"

"But what of all the other days that came before today? Where are they?" she asked with a bewildered look on her face.

"They're behind us. Or maybe in front of us. Who knows? All that matters is today." said the White Rabbit.

"But I don't even know who I am today!"

"Think of it this way: you are the Queen of Hearts, and you rule this land. That's a good start, don't you think?"

Down the Rabbit Hole

"Am I? Well, I do suppose that is a very good start," she said, her smile returning.

"And as your subject, I am at your whim. What shall we make our first order of business?"

"Perhaps we should bake a bunch of cakes?" she asked with a cheeky smirk.

"Cakes may not be the best way to start. Why don't we come up with another plan together, on our way to your castle. Don't worry, Your Majesty, I will show you the way."

THE END

Acknowledgments

I would like to offer my heartfelt gratitude to the various people who have made this series possible over the years:

Rich Thomas, for giving me the space and confidence to develop a voice that was uniquely my own, and for seeing something in me I did not see myself. Without Rich's patience, guidance, vision, and encouragement I would have never written this series.

Alexis Banyon, for being my champion while she was at Disney, and for all her encouragement over the years.

Megan Ilnitzki and Megan Roth, for being incredible editors and a joy to work with.

My amazing editor, Jocelyn Davies. She and I have been on quite the adventure together over the years, and I am so thankful to her for everything she has done for this series, and for me—most especially for helping me to better realize my vision for these characters, and their stories.